ESMIRANA'S TRUNK

Tales of Mystery and Suspense

ESMIRANA'S TRUNK

Tales of Mystery and Suspense

By Mark Stattelman

Copywrite ©2020
By Mark Stattelman
All rights reserved

ISBN-13:9798633569056

Table of Contents

THE HAND	1
ESMIRANA'S TRUNK	33
INCONTROVERTIBLE EVIDENCE	47
NIGHT TRAIN	73
CLACKERS	87
COBRA'S DEMISE	105
THE EARLY ONES	159
MYRA'S WEDDING	183
FOOTPRINTS	199

THE HAND

(A Milo Bates, P. I. story—A case in which there is very little detection on Milo's part.)

There was a reflection, a shadow, moving gracefully above and off to Milo's right. He pulled his gaze from Jessie. She was swimming downward, away from him, not paying any attention. He looked up at the sleek and silent shadow. His jaw tensed nervously, and a sense of foreboding overtook his mind; A faint chill clung to his body just inside the wetsuit. The shadow suddenly flexed and darted, attacking. He couldn't tell what it was attacking. He glanced back toward Jessie. She still hadn't noticed the shark. Milo backed slowly down and away, working his way toward her as the shark circled. The shark slackened its pace, then darted in again. A dark cloud of blood spilled out into the water, colorless. A fish, Milo thought. Feeding time. He backed further away from the growing cloud. Jessie looked up from below. Milo held the speargun at the ready, watching upward. Something struck against his elbow, almost setting off the gun. The second shark had just passed him, brushing against him by accident, nudging him, passing, then seemingly realizing it had just gone by dinner. In a flash it swung back toward him, on the attack. In another flash it was pushed violently to the side, the third shark's teeth ripping into it, flipping it. They were both on the edge of the cloud, the second shark's entrails spilling out as they fought, attracting the first shark, and still others. Milo backed hurriedly away and down, almost in a frenzy, trying desperately not to panic, his body rebelling against everything he had ever been taught about sharks and diving.

Jessie had been waiting near a reef that rose upward from the ocean floor. The floor moved out a

The Hand

few yards and then dropped away into blackness. Milo finally reached her at the reef, expecting to see terror on her face. He couldn't see her face though, because she was looking at something, watching it descend. He only saw the back of her head as she swam toward the descending object. He reached out, swiping at her fin, missing her. He looked up. The sharks were still struggling, but the cloud was beginning to disperse and break away. There were now five or six sharks, as near as he could tell; the smallest ranging from about six feet to the largest, which appeared to be about eighteen feet in length.

Again, Milo turned to watch Jessie. He noticed what it was she was after. A hand. It floated down, moving slowly, gliding toward the dark crevice below. As Milo moved closer, following Jessie's lead, he got a better view. There was a wrist and part of a forearm, that was all; descending debris that had escaped the milieu above. To the wrist were attached the remains of ripped twine and tape. At the end of the twine, there was a portion of heavy brick, pulling the hand toward the dark abyss. Jessie grabbed, entangling the twine around her own wrist, pulling the descending hand toward her. Milo was beside her now. He knew it was her preoccupation with forensic science that overrode her fear of the sharks above. His own curiosity peaked. The dim, yellowish grey of the murky depth surrounded them, while the reef, teeming with life and color in want of light lie in sharp contrast. They hovered at the edge of the abyss, as what purported to be the ocean floor, a mere ledge, moved. Tiny schools of fish of various size and shape darted about. And other, almost colorless urchins scattered and scampered around like a magic carpet, lending eerily to the atmosphere. Life would continue in the depths, somehow diminishing man, belittling him. Nature wouldn't even bat an eye over the death of a man, any man, not even the one no longer attached to the wrist which dangled at the end of the twine which Jessie now gripped tightly.

She clasped the twine and held it taut as the hand floated freely above, the brick dangling below. Milo sawed at the twine with his knife. There was a piece of plastic bag clinging to the inside of where the twine was bound to the wrist. The twine broke and the brick fell. Milo and Jessie looked at each other, and then upward. Milo shook his head. They could not go swimming up to the surface with the hand.

The Hand

The sharks wouldn't allow it. Hand or no hand, they wouldn't make it to the surface, Milo thought.

They could only see one or two dim shadows circling above now. They waited. One shadow darted off, then ten seconds later the other one was gone. Still, they couldn't be sure. It would probably be too risky. Milo looked at the gauges; The tanks had some air left, but they had been down for a while. They had about three or four minutes before they would have to ascend. He had a little less air than Jessie, due to his exertions earlier.

Jessie shook her head, motioning to him. The hand swayed back and forth in the water as she motioned. She was pointing at the fingers of her left hand with her right and then at the hand which floated magically at the end of twine. There were two rings on the floating hand one was a pinky ring and the other a wedding band. Up until that point, Milo had just assumed that it was a man's hand, but now he was almost certain. It was a large hand, though things always did appear larger under water.

Milo nodded his head. He understood. Or so he thought. He was under the impression that Jessie was going to pull the rings off and only take those up, but he was mistaken. She grabbed her knife out of its scabbard and began sawing at the fingers. He glanced nervously up toward where the sharks had been. Jessie followed his gaze. She was nervous also, but continued cutting the fingers. There was almost no blood. A very small thread floated out at first, but died away in tiny droplets. This was still probably enough to draw the keen senses of a shark, a hungry one. But Milo was hoping the local appetites had been satiated. They both looked up again, as if waiting for a shark to come down and attack. She shrugged and continued working. One finger came off, then a second. The third had the wedding band, and it almost dropped away when the finger was removed. Milo grabbed the ring in time. The water made motions slow, but slow motions are often clumsy motions. He saved the ring and Jessie dropped the finger. It landed on Milo's fin, and he steadied it enough until he could boot it up again, where he could reach out for it. The finger came up in a swirl of water and sand and then drifted just out of his reach. He floated, still and steady, straining his eyes to watch it closely, as though it were a small diamond. And so it can be likened, when it is compared to the surrounding ocean. It was a very miniscule thing, just as the man's life of which it

The Hand

had once been a part. The dim background and swaying plant life of the reef almost caused him to lose sight--There, he spotted it. It floated down and came to rest in a small crevice, as though pointing out a sea crab to Milo. He took out his knife and flicked the finger out, careful to grab it as it twirled free.

Milo turned back to Jessie. He glanced at his watch and the air pressure gauge. It was past time to start up. Jessie wasn't paying him any attention. He swam slowly to her and tugged on her arm pointing at his watch and motioning that they needed to ascend. She nodded. A large Grouper swam past them, but neither Jessie nor Milo even noticed. Milo saw that she had put the fingers in her mesh bag to carry up. He pointed at the bag and shook his head. He couldn't be sure the sharks were gone. Maybe he was overreacting, but better safe than sorry. He pointed to the side, velcro, pockets on the wetsuits. On the way up, they worked the fingers individually into each small, neoprene pocket. One of the fingers dropped, and drifted away. There was no way they could go back for it; there wasn't time. As it was, Milo was close to being out of air. They had their eyes wide open as they rose, looking in wide circles through the narrow view of the masks. The shadow of a Stingray passed overhead, but there were no signs of the sharks. They spotted the anchor line, and swam toward it, rising slowly, stopping every few feet to adjust to the change in pressure. They were still thirty feet from the surface when Milo ran out of air. He used the alternate, "octopus" regulator attached to Jessie's tank and followed her up. Only one thought flashed through Milo's mind just before they broke the surface. Sharks might not be the only danger. Suppose someone was waiting for them on deck?

They broke the surface and were blinded by the bright afternoon sunlight. The air tanks suddenly became leaden once out of the water, the heavy hand of gravity pulling them down, large fingers, grasping them, trying to pull them back into the depths from which they had just emerged. Waves splashed against them and lapped the side of the boat as they climbed aboard, water gushing and dripping from their wetsuits. They plopped onto the deck and started removing gear. Already the heat was becoming oppressive. The bright sunlight blinded them; and other than a fine mist of salty spray which rose up into the breeze as the boat

The Hand

rocked, they were quickly drying. There was only the squelching wetness of the suits as they tried to squirm out of them. Salty beads of sweat rose with the exertions.

Jessie had managed to get out of hers with an ease that always astounded Milo. How could she do it? He always cursed the damn things. He stopped to catch his breath, wanting to lie back on the deck and take a nap. He knew he would fry in the suit though if he did. Taking a deep breath of salty air, he started pulling again.

"Jesus," Milo said. "Those shar--" The boat rose up on a small wave, and he noticed something out of the comer of his eye. There was another boat in the distance, seemingly heading away. He didn't know if it was the one that had just dropped the man's body overboard, but it was highly likely. It would have to have been that or a helicopter, and he didn't see any birds whatsoever in the area. He looked around. He had looked when they were first climbing aboard to make sure there were no surprises waiting on deck for them. All seemed clear. They must have dropped the body and run. They had probably thought it was real cute to drop it where there were other divers, the man's pockets full of chum. Plenty of shark food to go around. Even if the divers had seen anything, they would not live to tell. After all, if they did live, there was still no evidence. Ha Ha. But they had been wrong. Evidence there was.

Milo glanced over at Jessie. She was already at work sorting and looking over that evidence at this very moment. She was bent down on the afterdeck, her chin-length blonde hair pushed back behind her ear. It fell forward again, wet tips grazing her salty cheek as she lay the fingers out on a towel. He guessed she couldn't stop being the forensic scientist any more than he could stop being a detective.

Milo began to wonder if maybe the crew who dumped the body deliberately dumped it where he was diving. Maybe an old case come back to haunt him. Maybe a coincidence, or maybe simple paranoia on his part. Maybe a lot of things. He glanced back at the boat. If he could only read the name of the boat. At this distance, no way. Maybe with the binoculars. He stood up and started below decks, glancing back at the pile of fins and scuba gear sitting loose on the deck. Bad idea, he thought, knowing full well he should secure that before anything else. Usually, Jessie was a real stickler on that aspect of diving, but not now. Now she was too

The Hand

wrapped up in her find. It'll hold for a couple minutes, thought Milo. It would also be a bad idea to let that boat get away without at least trying to identify it. They would have some explaining to do when they reached shore. Best to find out anything he could. Maybe he could still make out the name? If he could get that, then maybe he could contact the Coast Guard by radio and arouse enough suspicion so they would board and search her. "Can you bring me some freezer baggies, Milo?"

"Yeah, sure. Formaldehyde too?"

"Huh? No." She turned with a puzzled look on her face. She was squatted down with her back and right side turned toward him, peering at him over her right knee. "I don't need to preserve them--not in that way, I mean. That would destroy all the--" She stopped and smirked.

"Evidence." He knew what she meant. He just asked stupid questions sometimes to see how far into it all she really was. He continued down the ladder into the galley, glancing to where he had last hung the binoculars. He reached for them and a gun smashed across the side of his face hard enough to almost shatter his left cheek bone. He crumpled to the deck and blacked out, hitting his temple on the centerboard on the way down.

When Milo came to, there was a flash of bright light. He heard voices. The blazing sun was setting him on fire. He lay on the open deck, still encased in the now-dry wetsuit. Perspiration streamed down his face, his hair soaking wet with it. His head hurt and his body was on fire. He squeezed his eyes shut and opened them again, rolling to his side and wanting to vomit. The wave of nausea passed momentarily and he tried to remember what happened before lights out. Gradually, it came back to him. The other boat, the binoculars, the brick wall in the galley that he had run into.

The man must have been left behind to finish off anyone who happened to come out of the water alive after they dumped the body. He must have grown bored, maybe a little disgruntled at being the one left behind. Of course, the boat would be coming back to pick him up. No one could possibly escape the sharks; the man must have thought. He decided to go down and grab a tall, cool Killian's Red from the ice box below. He would come back up and check it out in a minute or two. He just wanted a cold one. That must have been his mistake.

The Hand

Milo and Jessie had climbed back on board and he was trapped below. They would see him coming up the ladder. It was the only way out. His only move was to wait until someone came down into the galley, or else the other boat came back to pick him up. That would distract them enough, and he could sneak up from behind. Milo accommodated him nicely though, by stepping below for the binoculars. The man didn't even have to wait all that long before Milo came down. Real sweet.

Milo ran his tongue across his lips and tasted blood. His face and the side of his head were aching. He rolled and tried to sit up. His wrists were tied, the hot wetsuit burning his hands where they rested against the front of it. Sitting up just enough, he could see them. His vision blurred and he almost passed out, but the image lingered:

Two people standing on the deck, near the port side, the same side where he and Jessie had come aboard after the shark attack. The two people were standing very close to each other, right on the edge of the deck. Milo was sure one of the two was Jessie. The boat swayed and rocked beneath him. A wave of nausea passed over him again and once again disappeared. The image became clear. The man's smile was the first thing Milo noticed. He was leering, his teeth were trimmed in gold. He glanced at Milo once, but there seemed to be no fear in his eyes. After all, what harm could a half-groggy man who was on the deck with his hands tied together do?

The man with Jessie was young, early twenties, and appeared to be Cuban, but Milo wasn't sure. Jessie's hands were tied behind her back, probably so he could have easy access to her. He was very close to her, and he moved his hand to her bikini bottoms, running his fingers along the inner elastic. His grin widened and he leaned in close to her face.

Milo closed his eyes again for a second and opened them, trying to re-focus, trying to think. He reached down to the inside of his leg. His knife was gone. He continued to move, slowly managing to work his way to his knees, all the time watching the young Cuban and Jessie. He saw that her hands were tied off to one of the air tanks. Apparently, nothing heavier was handy. Milo could only see Jessie's profile, but he saw enough of it. Her eyes closed as the man stuck his hand deeper into her bikini bottoms. Then she opened her eyes and a severe hatred shone in them. Milo had never seen her project such a hatred before. This only seemed to excite the Cuban

The Hand

even more. He leaned in closer and brushed his lips against hers. She closed her eyes again and tried to turn away. The man licked her cheek and laughed out loud. He glanced at Milo and laughed. Jessie spit in his face and he stopped laughing and called her a bitch. He said something else in Spanish. He pulled his hand out of her bikini and Milo saw that he had been stuffing chum into her pants. A bit of it fell to the deck. Milo somehow was on his feet. The man's hand swiped across Jessie's cheek leaving a trail of the chum across her face. Some of the chum flung off his hand and went flying into the sun, spattering against the bright yellow background before dropping into the ocean. Milo was running towards them, the deck swaying beneath him. He felt as though he was running with all of his might, but it was more of a stumble. He had the image of moving in slow motion, as in a dream.

Just as the man pushed her over, Jessie turned. She was close enough. And he had also been distracted by Milo coming at them. She had grabbed the man's belt and pulled him with her. She was trying for the knife he had in his belt, in the front. He was going for it at the same time, though his intention was to use it on Milo after he pushed her over the side. He hadn't seen her hand. She had been quick to turn, too quick. He shouldn't have been so close to her. They both went, just as the knife twisted up into his stomach.

Milo was inches from reaching them when they went over the side. He had been moving groggily, staggering, stumbling, trying for their direction. Through bleary eyes, groggily, he watched them go, Jessie screaming as they plunged overboard. The air tank slid and clanged against the side of the deck before flipping over after them. Milo followed it over, his hands still tied in front of him. He hit the water rolling, and then straightening himself to a cutting edge, knifing downward. He spotted Jessie and the Cuban. They were gliding toward the depths.

Milo hooked himself between the two, struggling. Jessie still clung to the man's belt, mainly out of desperation. The knife was beginning to work loose from the man's stomach. Jessie had the hilt of it in her hand. The air tanks were pulling them towards bottom. The attached BCD was deflated. Milo pumped it up and that helped to slow the descent. It even started to suspend them, but not for long. He opened the valve on the tank, grabbed the regulator

The Hand

and worked it to Jessie's mouth. She cleared it, took a few breaths, and he let go, going for the octopus one. Fortunately, the man had chosen Jessie's tank from earlier, at least there was a little air left. He must not have known too much about diving, or he wouldn't have left the regulator, BCD and gauges attached before tying her off to it. He didn't have any more bricks, Milo guessed. But if you are trying to drown someone, you don't send them down with diving equipment. Of course, she was tied up.

Milo sensed the shark's approach before he saw it. He was becoming too used to this sort of thing. He hoped it wasn't habitual. He tried to maneuver the Cuban around between them and the approaching shark, but was having some difficulty. Of course, the man was dead, or should be, considering the way the knife was twisted up into him; Or perhaps the air tank had hit him in the head when it followed him and Jessie over. Milo couldn't tell for sure. He peeled Jessie's hands off the knife and pulled it free of the man. Milo was just cutting the rope around Jessie's hands free as the shark caught most of the Cuban. The man had a horrified look on his face, the gold teeth showing in a deathlike grin as the shark flung him from side to side. And then he was gone and there was only the shark's grin.

Milo remembered the chum in Jessie's pants, and he ripped them off of her. There had been no time for her to cut his hands free. The shark came at them; its cold, flat, steely eye staring. Milo raised the knife in both hands and brought the hilt of it down hard on the shark's snout as it came in to take a bite. It was momentarily stunned, but only slightly. The chum had fallen free of Jessie and some of it had lodged in between the top of the BCD and the one tank. Milo reached down and cut the hoses to the regulator, then stabbed at the BCD. The shark reacted, and veered in again. A second shark was already on the way, as a cloud of bubbles shot upward. Milo and Jessie moved off to the side of the stream of air bubbles, trying to get away. Milo had read somewhere that sharks could sometimes be distracted by a cloud of air bubbles; the bubbles, at least in theory, perhaps were from a frantic human, or fish, or whatever type of dinner, trying to get away. There was never any guarantee with sharks in the midst of a feeding frenzy. Milo had been surprised that he was able to stun the first shark with the blow to the snout with the knife hilt.

The Hand

It worked. Jessie and Milo sat very still in the water, trying to cease all movement, and yet stay afloat. Both of their lungs were about to burst from lack of air. Jessie worked at the rope holding Milo's hands together. They were moving toward the surface as best they could when the line went taut connecting Jessie to the tanks. The third shark shot in and grabbed the chum, along with tanks and all, in one bite as the other two dived after it. All the sharks were confused by the bubbles; and jessie was frantically pulled downward in one fantastic jolt. Her last breath escaped her throat in a small bubble of air. Milo could have sworn that he had cut the rope. Apparently, he hadn't, not completely. The knife flipped out of her hands. She was immediately three feet away from it as her fingers clawed for its blade end. It was gone and she hadn't completely freed Milo's hands. She needed air, and it wasn't Milo's hands she was thinking about at the moment.

The sharks thrashed about below, pulling her back and forth. Milo lunged for the knife, missed and lunged again. Jessie had cut the rope enough after all; Some strenuous tugging on his part had broken the binding free from around his hands. He had to choose between Jessie and air. His lungs were shot.

Mark Stattelman

The flailing shark had thrashed about and snapped through the rope connecting Jessie to the tank. She was free. They both shot quickly for the surface. Milo's last glance over his shoulder before heading up, showed the shark that had swallowed the air tank being ripped apart by the others. Bubbles still escaped through the shark's mouth and floated upward. There must have been more air in the tank than Milo had thought. Or maybe only a couple of minutes had passed since the underwater ordeal had begun. Air, precious Air. Sharks or no sharks, they moved to the bubbles, hoping the rising air would help push them upward, Milo and Jessie hadn't been pulled that deep after all. They had just been down for what seemed like an eternity. They broke the surface.

The boat had drifted, but not by much. Milo and Jessie's lungs heaved in the fresh air as they swam toward it. Finally, only another eight feet to go. seven, six, five, four, three. . . two . . .one.

One hand on the ladder, two. Jessie was up, with Milo coming up fast behind her.

"Hello," said a voice somewhere in front of her on the deck, startling her. She looked up at the man moving toward her. She turned and looked down.

The Hand

The shark came up out of the water, jaws open wide, behind Milo. Something in between the two visions caught her eye. Something lying on the deck. She reached for it looking up at the man, then back down. She saw Milo swing his legs up out of the way as the shark bit through the ladder.

She fired. The man fell backward on the deck, the revolver he held fell from his hand. The spear stuck up out of the middle of his chest. There was no one else around. He was Cuban, a little older than the other one, probably a little smarter, but just as dead. The other boat drifted quietly along the starboard side. It had returned for the first man after all.

Milo rolled up and over onto the deck. He was bleeding. The last shark had gotten ahold of him. Not only had it caught the ladder, but it had also taken a small chunk of flesh from his thigh and buttocks. The pain was excruciating. He lay on his side, staring up at Jessie. She stood on the deck, half naked, staring down at the man she had killed.

She still held the spear gun in her left hand.

"Jessie," Milo groaned. She didn't move.

"Jessie," he tried again. Still she didn't move. Milo reached, grabbing her ankle. She jumped, startled. "Jessie!" She turned and finally looked down at

Milo. Her eye catching the spear gun. She turned slowly, still in a daze. She stared at the gun, then dropped it to the deck. Milo hollered again. She looked at him, her eyes vacant. He called to her, soothing his voice. "Jessie, come here." It took a few moments for his voice to register, but she eventually responded by coming over to him. She moved slowly, still in a daze. She was finally standing over him. "Down here," he said. "Bend down." Slowly, she squatted, staring at him. He grabbed her face in his hands and pulled her close. For a second, he grit his teeth against the pain in his backside. "Jessie, I'm hurt. You've got to get help." Still it didn't seem to register. He slapped her hard across the face, putting his pain into it. Her eyes watered with the slap, her head flinging to one side. She turned back to Milo, recognition seeping back into her face. She broke, tears flooding down her cheeks.

"M-Milo . . . I k-k-killed a m-ma-that m-man. Sh-shot . . . spear. . . I -kk--"

Milo shook her. She stopped talking, but the tears continued. "Jessie," he said, pausing. He decided it best not to tell her she had actually killed two men. "It doesn't matter. It had to be. It was--"

The Hand

"It matters," she stumbled on through tears. "Oh, it matters. It matters a lot." She started to rock back and forth, moving along with the boat.

"Okay, okay. It matters, but not right now." He reached up and pushed her hair back from her face with his thumb, looking her straight in the eyes, sincerely. She was suddenly a little girl again, not the twenty-four-year old that he had known and made love to many a night. The twenty-four-year old woman would be back, he was sure of it. A wiser, more mature, very old twenty-four, but she would be back. There was a big difference between studying the dead tissue of a body with a scientific eye, and actually bringing death to a living being with your own hand. "What matters right now is that you get a grip," he continued. "You need to get a hold on yourself Jessie. I'm hurt. I'm bleeding. I need a doctor. You've got to get the first aid kit. And you've got to radio for help. They will need to send a helicopter, probably." He looked at her. She stared back.

"Do you understand Jessie?" She nodded. Slowly, but she nodded. She understood. "Now, Jessie. Go radio for help and bring the first aid kit. Now. Please." She nodded again and got slowly to her feet. She moved toward the ladder leading below deck, only stopping to look back at Milo once, looking back over her shoulder. He smiled a painful smile at her as she pushed her hair back behind her ear absently, out of mere habit. She was very careful to keep her eyes turned away from the man lying on the deck with the spear sticking out of his chest. "And Jessie," Milo called after her. She was at the ladder and started down. She stopped and looked at him. "Get some shorts on, or something. Before they get here." She looked down at herself, just then realizing she was naked except for her bikini top. She disappeared below.

After she was gone, Milo crawled, pulling himself, inching slowly over to where the man lay on the deck. The spear stuck straight up out of the man's chest, and blood still seeped out around it through his shirt. It ran down his left side, and spilled over into a widening pool on the deck. Milo reached up and felt the man's throat. There was no pulse. He pulled himself over to the man's firearm, which lay silently on the deck, not more than three feet away. Milo picked it up and gripped it tightly in his hand. He knew it would have been too much to ask Jessie to come close enough to the man to pick the gun up before going down below. Even though it would

The Hand

have been for her own safety, he couldn't bring himself to suggest it. He did, however decide that he would watch the entrance below with a sharp eye, and if anyone came up out of there besides her, or even with her, he would not hesitate to fire. After all, he had been ambushed below, and there was no way of knowing whether there were other men besides the two they had come across. The other boat sat silent, rocking in the water. Milo cranked his head around and took a quick glance at it. No signs of anyone stirring on it as far as he could tell. His neck grew stiff. He looked away and tried to roll over so he could get a better view of the door to the galley when the time came for Jessie to emerge. He wondered what could be taking her so long. He knew he would have to somehow edge away from the man on the deck before she came back up. She would have a hard time coming to administer first aid to him when the man she had just killed lie right beside him. He would move away in a second, he thought. He just needed to lie back and rest. Just for a moment.

***

When Milo woke up again there was a dim light all around. He sucked in quickly, trying to pull air from the regulator. There wasn't one. He panicked, thinking he might drown. Then he realized that the air was coming free and easy. He could breathe. He felt around and touched bed sheets. His hand knocked against the railing of the hospital bed. He looked to his left and saw Jessie. She was perched in a chair beside the bed, reading a book. She looked over at him and smiled, reaching over to touch his forehead.

"How you feeling?"

Milo thought about it for a second. "A little lighter in the rear, but other than that, like a million bucks."

"Don't worry. You only lost about ten pounds back there. You're just about right now." She smiled. "Really, it wasn't as bad as you thought. They did have to do some patch work though, from what I hear. I haven't really seen it since they stitched you up. They keep it pretty well bandaged." She decided not to tell him just yet that she had done most of the initial sewing back at the boat, using a needle and some fishing line. She had concentrated on the sewing. It was the only thing keeping her terror under control, sitting there on the deck with the man she

The Hand

had killed only two feet away. "You probably aren't feeling much pain right now, huh?."

"Not really. How long's it been?"

"About four days."

"Where am I?"

"Miami General."

"The boat?"

"Back in Velo Beach. Your usual parking slip at the pier."

"They find out who the hand belongs to?"

"Yeah, you remember the guy down from New York? From that Real Estate syndicate? The one who disappeared after trying to buy up all that waterfront property along South Beach?"

"Yeah, it was in all the papers that he mysteriously disappeared and it was real weird that Ricardo Avio immediately bought up all of it." Ricardo Avio was a local, Velo Beach, heavy hitter. He was into drug smuggling mostly, but also whatever else turned a buck. He was suddenly into Real Estate. "I thought that land was contaminated. That's why the guy disappeared? I know they had been trying to play it off as though he flew quietly on back to New York."

"Well it turns out that the land wasn't quite as contaminated as they thought at first. That had just been a ploy to bring the price down. Anyway, the guy hadn't gone back to New York, because it was his body that was dumped overboard by the thugs on the other boat. Guess who the boat was chartered for? What name?"

"Avio?"

"You guessed it."

Milo shook his head. "Why would he be that stupid?"

"Maybe he thought his men were smart enough to go far enough out to dump the body."

"Or I guess he didn't realize they had a sick enough sense of humor to dump the thing where people were diving. They thought they had the situation under control by sticking around to make sure no one came up alive."

Jessie squirmed a little in the chair.

"So you were able to get finger prints from the fingers we brought up?"

"Well, yeah, but they weren't much help at first. They didn't seem to match up with any on file. The guy had never been convicted of anything. He was clean. Then the wife came down looking for him. She identified the rings. She said he had been in the military at some point, so somebody got a hold of a

The Hand

clerk somewhere, but they couldn't find his file. The woman said she thought he might have a copy back home in a file cabinet with a lot of military papers. Her sister went over and dug, and tracked down a copy of his prints for us. Actually, we would have probably only needed the folder itself, or any copy of a letter, just something we could dust for prints, something he had touched. But the actual documented prints are better.

"The twine and then fibers and skin fragments under the nails helped to determine who actually killed him. There were traces from the boat he was dumped off of, the trunk of a car, which also led to Avio . . ."

Milo interrupted her: "So the salty water really didn't damage the fingers much?"

"No, they weren't down there long enough. We just had to sort out some of the materials. There were bits of neoprene, of course, from our suits. That sort of thing."

"Yeah, I was thinking about that back on the boat. I should have let you keep the things in the dive bag, away from our bodies, that was really stupid. At least we could have dropped the bag if we were attacked . . ."

"Well . . ."

"Anyway," Milo went on. "We gotta give the guy a hand for solving his own murder." He realized what he had said after he said it and saw the pained look on Jessie's face.

"Please," she said.

"Bad joke, huh?"

"Very."

They both smirked.

"The boat and the man, were strong points of evidence. And if it hadn't been for the two of us diving, the men dropping him on top of where we were diving . . ."

"Amazing," Milo said. "They really could have dropped him anywhere else in the ocean and gotten away clean. We go diving and I get a case dropped right in my hands." "Our hands," she corrected him. She gasped. "And will you quit with the hand jokes. That's sick."

"You're doing it too." He smiled at her. "Besides, I'm the only licensed detective here."

"And you can keep it too. I don't want any part in it."

The Hand

Milo knew what she was talking about. He noticed earlier that she had made reference to the boat and the 'man', not the dead man. There was a silence.

"So how are you doing?" he asked. She knew what he meant.

She squirmed and looked away. A few more seconds passed before she answered.

"Let's just say I won't be doing any diving with you again for a while. Come to think of it, you won't be doing much diving either." She reached over to the bed and pushed the rail down, then sat on the bed beside him. "Let me see those stitches, anyway."

"Maybe later," he said.

She leaned down and kissed him.

"Definitely later," he corrected as their lips parted.

ESMIRANA'S TRUNK

Esmirana and I had known each other since we were children. She was five and I was seven when her folks moved in next door. Her father was a military man, as was mine. They had even served with the same regiment in the Falklands, though at different times. They had just more or less missed each other at various times. When one was just graduating Sandhurst, the other was beginning.

***

"Come, I want to show you something," said the dark-haired little girl as she grabbed my hand and led me to the small garden in the courtyard. Her eyes were all aglow with excitement as she looked at me when she pulled me to her spot.

"What?"

"But don't you see it? It's beautiful!"

"What?"

She would point then. It was a grasshopper the first time. Another time a cocoon from which emerged a butterfly after several days of watching. There was always something. Something exciting to her. Something about life itself. Always. As she grew older, she shared other things with me. At eleven, she showed me a time capsule she was going to bury. It was just a small tin with a few items. She made me promise that I wouldn't tell anyone what the contents were, ever. My lips are sealed to this day. Though I am quite sure the small tin has been unearthed, or perhaps simply rusted away to nothing, its contents lost to future generations. Then it was astronomy. After that, painting. It went on and on . . .

"Come, I want to show you something . . ."

Esmirana's Trunk

Though we grew up together, there was a lot I still did not know about her. I didn't know that she had a heart condition until she was about thirteen or so. It was only in passing that I found out. I believe my mother mentioned it over dinner one evening. I remember going to hospital to visit. We couldn't get in to see her. They said she was resting. She had an enlarged heart, and would require frequent periods of rest.

We drifted apart, Esmirana and I, different interests, age difference, etc. I barely thought of her. I would come home for the holidays and maybe see her in passing. She would wave and smile, but that would be it.

I didn't notice her again until after I had returned from college. I ran into her at the local market and we rode the tube home together. It was rather pleasant. We chatted a bit. I hadn't realized how beautiful she had grown until just then. It was her reflection in the tube window that I noticed, her dark and shining hair, her flashing dark eyes. Her reflection caught me looking and smiled back, a slight blush appearing on her cheeks.

"I want to show you something," she said. "At the next stop." When we got to the next stop, I had to ask her to point out whatever it was she had meant. "See that man over there, the one on the bench?"

"The one in the worn brown coat?"

"Yes."

"He is asleep."

"Yes. Every day, at this same time, on this same bench.

"And?"

"And, well . . ." She hesitated

"Well?"

"You don't see it do you?"

"What?"

"Oh, nothing. Really. It's just that I seem to see things differently than others. Perhaps more than others."

"Hm."

"Don't do that."

"What?"

"Patronize me."

"I'm not."

"Okay, all I was going to say was that we are all sort of like that man. We are all sleeping through life. We don't see things . . ." She said this hurriedly, as though it wasn't what she truly meant. At least

Esmirana's Trunk

not exactly, not totally. She turned and saw me grinning at her. "Shut up," she said.

"What? You have grown into quite the philosopher while I've been away!"

"Just. Shut up." She was grinning.

I was in love, and so was she. From that moment on we both knew it. It was a most joyful walk home from the tube that evening.

Neither of our parents wanted us to marry. On the side of mine I suspect a small bit of prejudice. Esmirana's great grandmother had been Hindu. Though Esmirana was white as alabaster, she still maintained a dark, bewitching beauty of eyes and hair that would make her suspect. Her parents had their own reasons for not wanting the union to take place. Perhaps they thought I wasn't worthy of her, or perhaps it was a fear for her health?
In retrospect, they would have been correct in fearing for her health.

***

The honeymoon was an extended cruise to Jamaica. We were unable to fly due to Esmirana's heart condition. I continually tried to persuade her to rest. Sometimes I was successful in the attempt.

She looked rested, happy. We were both overjoyed at our luck in finding each other. We had known each other for years, but both felt that we had only just met. We were finding out new surprises each day about each other. Our future was bright.

"Come, I want to show you something," Esmirana said. We had been about fifteen or twenty minutes, rummaging in a small Jamaican shop. It was a sort of thrift, junk shop, sort of place. I was looking at what appeared to be a small nautical instrument of some sort, nothing spectacular, when Esmirana tugged at my sleeve. I believe it was something else she was headed for when the trunk caught her attention. "Ooh, honey, look at this. Isn't it fantastic? We can store our trinkets in here, anything we buy, and drag it aboard ship. Then ninety years from now, we can open it up and remember everything about our honeymoon."

"Last night wasn't memorable enough for you?"

"You know what I mean," she smirked. "The rest of our trip." I was reminded of the time capsule she had buried as a little girl. "We can use it for other things too, our hopes and dreams, all of our precious treasures, our whole future. . . We can even

Esmirana's Trunk

use it as a crib for our first born, and perhaps our second, or third . . ." She grinned at me.

"Well, I guess we'll take it," I said, turning to the proprietor. She was a dark lady with a wide grin, full of island flavour. "Who can resist?"

"Oh, dat's a beauty. She is no?"

I wasn't sure whether she meant Esmirana or the trunk. The trunk didn't seem all that special. I heard the thud and turned. The woman shrieked, and I'm not sure I didn't do the same. I ran to my wife. It was hopeless. Esmirana lay draped across the trunk. She was dead.

***

It has been two years since her death and still she haunts my every waking minute; though not as you might imagine. Oh, I miss her. I truly do, terribly. But let me explain. It is the trunk. The trunk is the thing which holds more evil than you can imagine, than can be fathomed by anyone. My shrink thinks I am totally crazy. I'm surprised he hasn't committed me yet. It must only be compassion on his part. He feels that I am deeply upset about the death of my wife, and he is correct. Little does he realize the truth of it--that there is more, oh, so much more!

***

It started subtly, slowly, while I was still in the throes of mourning. I would dream about her, yearn for her. In that misty, dreamlike state she would call to me . . . "Come, I want to show you something." The voice would be hers. I was sure of it. At least at first. I would hear the voice, her voice, calling to me. From. . . From the trunk. I know it sounds crazy, but it is the truth. I would hear her voice and follow it to the closed trunk. I could hear her inside, but couldn't open the lid. "Come," she would say. "I want to show you something." I tried with all my might to open it. I tried to prise the lid up, but it would not budge, not even a fraction of an inch. In despair, as I had tried everything that I could think of to open it; I collapsed on the edge of the bed. All of a sudden it opened of its own accord. It opened easily; The lid just stood up by itself, open wide. I lunged at it, looking within, nothing. It was completely empty. Nothing remarkable about an empty trunk. Nothing remarkable at all. No. At least not unless your wife's voice happens to be coming from within. Your dead wife. But the voice was no longer coming as I stood looking down into the box. I thought at this point that I truly must have lost my mind. I closed the trunk lid and immediately the next day made an appointment with a shrink.

The psychologist lulled me into thinking it was all just stress, my weary mind playing tricks. I agreed wholeheartedly. In the clear light of day, sitting there in his office, it made sense. It was all just an illusion. My wife's death had been traumatic for me to say the least. We had just started our life together. Why did she have to die just then, just when we were beginning to live?

I went home depressed, but feeling quite sane. Yes, it had been my mind, overwrought nerves, whatever. I was fine, more or less.

That night was quite peaceful. Nothing happened. Even the second night was serene. But the third was when it all began again. I was lying in the semi-awake state just before drifting off to sleep when I heard my wife calling me: "Come, I want to show you something."

I sat bolt upright, not sure whether I had dreamed it or whether it was actually coming from the trunk again (or my mind). I waited. Silence. I continued to wait, frozen in a sitting position, unable to move. Still silence. I sat for three or four minutes, muscles tense. Nothing. I waited. I felt the tenseness of my muscles and since all seemed quiet, I relaxed; just a little at first, then a little more. Still only silence filled the room. I eased back down, ready to concede that my mind was playing tricks again. I breathed a big sigh of relief. Relax, I thought. Breathe in and out, slowly. I took another calm breath, relaxing even more. . . Silence lingered, giving way only to the sound of my own breathing.

"Come, I want to show you something."

"Wha--"

"Come, I want to show you something."

I trembled, rising from the bed onto wobbly legs, weak with fear. It was definitely my wife's voice, somewhat muffled, yet distinct and clear to a fantastic degree. I had heard her say these words many times. It was her voice. I took two steps toward the trunk, which was about twelve feet away. The lid started to lift, slowly, of its own accord. Bony fingers belonging to the hand of death pushing the lid up would have not been any more of a shock. It was this thought that froze me in my tracks. I felt a chill. What would appear? The lid continued to rise.

"Come, I want to show you something."

Esmirana's Trunk

The words came again, distinctively clear, definitely my wife's, yet not. There was something behind them, not forcing them, but propping the words up, so to speak, filling me with a trepidation chilling me completely. I lunged for the door of the room, but was repelled backwards almost immediately. It was as though a cool breeze had blown between me and the door, a breeze of tremendous force, something not human, unclean, evil. There was nothing there that I could see. I felt it, however, this great, vile force. The trunk lid continued to slowly rise, but there was nothing else visible happening in the room. There was a definite palpable feeling of evil about the room though. I watched, unable to move. Something did begin to rise from the trunk then, a misty substance which took the form of my wife. I stared, perplexed, fascinated, transfixed. I watched as the apparition took shape. It truly was Esmirana. She smiled. She unfurled a finger, beckoning me, curling it inward, then unfurling it again. Again, she curled it, smiling. A sweet, seductive smile. Her dark eyes seemed aglow with a sultry mist, love. I took two steps toward her. "Come," she said softly. "I want to show you something." Two more steps and I was closer to her. With outstretched arms she beckoned me, calling me by name. Another step and I was within her embrace. Her fingers curled grasping at my shoulders. Her face was close to mine. "Come," she said seductively. "I want to show you something . . ." She smiled. Her lips were parting, red. Her breath, pulling me in toward her, close enough that it seemed to be sucking my own, out of my mouth, air out of the very depth of my lungs. I had difficulty breathing. It was then that I felt a tugging at my pants legs. I looked down. Snakes, a swarm of them slithering where her feet should be in the bottom of the trunk. There is no bottom, only a dark abyss. I am dreamily aware that they are slithering up over the sides of the trunk and are sliding smoothly up my legs. They are at my ankles, slithering coldly up my shins, wrapping around my calves, pulling me toward them. They are more like fingers, coldly pulling, tugging at my legs, continually pulling, gently at first, then with more force. I try to step up and away, back from them. I look up again. Esmirana's red lips are parted, curling upward and back, still sucking my breath, my very life. I struggle to pull away. The lips part further, the bony teeth become more visible, the smile wide. The putrid stench of death overcomes me. The hands grasping my shoulders are strong and digging into my flesh. Mere bones, like pincers; my wife's flesh has gone I know not where. She has withered before my eyes and become Cali herself. A strange cackle escapes the thing. I struggle to free myself. I pray with all of my heart, I plead. I call out to Esmirana to have pity on me, to let me live. "Please." Whatever it is that has me in its grip loosens a little, falteringly. It hesitates. Slowly, it recedes and I collapse to the floor.

  This was only one such episode. There have been others. I have tried to have the trunk hauled away. Each time it is returned to me in some fashion. Once a man said a beautiful young lady with dark hair and dark eyes paid him to deliver it to my address. Other times it just appears. I have given up trying to get rid of it, at least until I figure out a way. At times, late at night I will awaken and feel something caressing me, nudging, coaxing me toward where the thing stands open. In terror, I am jolted upright out of sleep, wondering whether it is but a dream. Other times I am awakened by someone weeping, sitting on the edge of my bed. It appears to be my wife; but when I reach for her shoulder to comfort her, she turns and I know that something isn't quite right. I know it isn't really her. At least not wholly her.

***

Well, the doctor has formally requested that I stay here at the hospital. Nothing permanent, he said. That was the day before yesterday.

Yesterday he came into my room and walked me to the trunk. He had intended on flipping the lid open to show me that nothing was inside. The trunk would not open. He insisted that I had locked it and was hiding a key somewhere. He demanded that I open the thing. Today, maybe it will open. "Come," he says. "I want to show you something." There is something in his voice. Oh, not that he sounds like my wife. It isn't that. I know better. Still, I pause and look at him suspiciously. I wonder whether it will open for him today. A part of me hopes it will, but another part of me dreads that it might. Slowly, we move toward it . . .

INCONTROVERTIBLE EVIDENCE

"What?"
"That's what I said."
"What, that you would kill her?"
"Yeah, if I ever saw her again."

The two men looked at where the woman's body lie slumped over on the floor, her head and one shoulder wedged up against the front of the couch, the edge of the coffee table overhanging her left hip. She could have merely been sleeping, but would have had one stiff neck when she woke up. As it was, from the angle of her slumped head, her neck appeared to be broken.

The two men stood looking down at her. One man, whose name was Leonard, was shorter, dumpier than the other. The taller one, Michael, had a stooped, tired look about him. He had a weary, bags under the eyes look. His arms were lanky; and in spite of all his tiredness, when he spoke, he moved his arms and hands in sweeping gestures, which gave him a certain cartoonish animation.

"So you said you were gonna kill her?" Leonard said, clearing his throat before speaking.

"Yeah, how many times have I got to repeat myself?"

Leonard sighed, reached in his pocket for a pack of smokes, Lucky Strikes. He held out the pack to Michael. Michael just looked at him. Leonard took a cigarette out and lit it, turning away from Michael, walking a few paces toward a sliding glass door leading out onto a balcony. He stood looking out. Dusk was approaching. There was a reddish orange glow in the sky that was rising up around the edges of the smog and beginning to turn just a hint of purple. It was going to be a beautiful sunset. He turned and looked back at the taller man. The sun's dying rays, shining from behind him, caught the side of his face as he turned, highlighting one of his pockmarked cheeks, and accentuated the hollows of his eyes. If what he saw when he turned around startled him, he didn't show it. Michael was down on his hands and knees, peering intently at the dead woman's face. "Michael," he said. The man didn't respond. He waited a minute, watching. Michael just kept staring at the woman's face. "Michael—what in the hell are you doing"

Michael looked up at him with a blank yet very pale look on his face. "God she is gorgeous. Was, I mean. Jesus, Leonard I can't believe she's dea--" He swallowed hard, looking back at the woman. "Dead. I just can't fucking believe it. You know." He sat back on his legs and watched her, his head pivoting in different positions, much like a pigeon getting ready to peck at a small morsel of grain.

"You gonna be okay kid?"

Michael got up and started pacing the floor, nervously biting the left side of his lip. His dirty blonde hair hung down in a long strand in front of his face. His cheekbones were high, and gave a gaunt, sallow look to his face. "Yeah," he mumbled. He looked nervously around, plopped onto the edge of a chair, laced his long fingers together, then untwined them and stood up again.

"You sure?"

Michael ignored him. He was pacing again. He sighed, loud and heavy. He moved his head from one side to the other as though trying to relieve a crick in his neck. Leonard just looked on, a half inch of ash dangling from the cigarette in his mouth. All at once Michael started hyperventilating. He sat quickly onto the edge of the chair again and stuck his head between his legs. The ash dropped from Leonard's cigarette.

Leonard pulled the cigarette from his mouth and blew out a cloud of smoke. "You sick? Want something? A bucket, or pan or something?"

Michael mumbled something from between his legs. Leonard didn't quite hear what it was.

"What?"

Michael raised his head a little. "Scotch."

"Scotch?"

"Yeah, in the cabinet." He pointed to his left, to a small cabinet resting against the wall across the room from the couch. Leonard walked over to it, opened one of the bottom doors and pulled out a

Incontrovertible Evidence

bottle of J&B from a lower shelf. There were pictures on the top of the cabinet, framed pictures of the woman and various relatives. Leonard picked up one of the framed pictures of the woman and looked closely at it. The woman was beautiful. He looked behind him at where the body lie on the floor. A damn shame, he thought. He turned and looked at Michael, holding up the bottle. Michael peeked up over his left leg. Tears were running down his face. Leonard decided not to ask about the glasses, realizing they would be in the kitchen. He put his cigarette out in a small ashtray on top of the cabinet and disappeared around the corner, wishing Michael had called someone else instead of him.

"You sure you wouldn't rather have coffee?" Leonard hollered from the kitchen. "Be a hell of a lot easier dealing with the cops . . ." He wondered what was taking them so long to get there. He was hoping he could leave soon enough after they arrived. They would have to ask him some questions too, of course. He would just tell it like it was. Michael had called him and asked him to come over. He seemed upset over the phone and said he had "a problem." It wasn't until Leonard had arrived that Michael told him what the problem was, and by that time it was too late to turn around and leave. He would tell the police that he had only known Michael for the last six months or so, which was about how long Michael had been working down at the office. Hell, maybe it was seven or eight months. Something like that. He thought back. It had been before Labor Day. He was sure of that. Michael had been at the barbecue. Yeah, that's the first time he had really talked to him. And then they had gone for drinks a couple of times after work. Nothing much. It's not like they had been real close buddies or anything. He had liked the kid okay, sure. He seemed like a decent enough guy, a little odd sometimes, but nothing in particular, nothing Leonard could put his finger on. "How about that coffee? You want I should put some on just in case?" There wasn't any response from the other room. Hell. Guess not. The cops would be hanging out and drinking coffee, taking their sweet ass time with the whole thing. He didn't want to be here half the night answering questions. He pulled a couple of glasses from the cupboard and filled one with the scotch. He held it under the tap and eased a little cool water, just a splash, into the glass, then leaned back against the counter and took a large swallow. He thought about if he had to give a character reference to them about Michael, sort of a profile. What would he say? He wasn't quite sure? Could the kid have killed her? He didn't think so. Hell, he didn't think the kid had much in the way of balls when it came down to it. He was always sort of an artsy fartsy type. Not in any phony way, though. The kid didn't broadcast it or anything, didn't put on airs. Nothing like that. You could tell he was educated though, somewhere back east. Far from broadcasting though. The kid seemed aloof, yeah, that was what he was looking for, the word. No, hell no. *Aloof* would sound like he could have done it. He wasn't out to make the kid look guilty. The killer would have been aloof. Some sort of loner. The killers in these cases were always loners, "aloof, psychopathic." Low-key, yeah, that was it. The kid low-key. He had kept a low profile, not saying much.

Leonard tried to remember whether the kid had even mentioned having a wife before now. Yeah, well, seems like the kid had mentioned something about a divorce. The first time they had been out for drinks, down at Murphy's. That was it. Maybe. Leonard wasn't exactly sure. He couldn't remember much of anything substantial about the guy. But he seemed like a good kid all the same.

Leonard took another drink and then poured some scotch into the second glass. He got a few cubes from the icebox and put them in both glasses. The ice clinked against the sides of the tumblers when he dropped them in, and some of the liquid splashed out onto the counter. Things seemed awful quiet. He wondered if maybe the kid had cried himself to sleep in just the short time he had been in the kitchen. "Hey, kid," he hollered out. The silence made him nervous. He rounded the corner into the living room. Hey, Michael, you okay?" The guy wasn't there.

Leonard heard the sounds coming from the bathroom even before he was halfway down the hall. Michael was in there throwing up. Leonard put his ear to the door. Sure enough. He rapped on the door with his knuckles, lightly. "Hey, you okay?

"Yeah," a weak voice answered back. Then came more of the heaving, vomiting sounds. Leonard eased away from the door and went back down the hall to the living room. He plopped down onto the chair that Michael had been in earlier, taking out another cigarette and lighting it. He took a long drag and sat back. The leather of chair creaked beneath him as he settled back. He picked up his drink from where he had set the two on the coffee table, glancing at the body on the floor a couple of feet away. It looked like the body had been moved, only slightly, but he wasn't quite sure. He took a big swallow of scotch and set the glass down. He eased off the chair and got down for a closer look at the woman's body. Maybe she's not completely dead, he thought. He didn't want to, but he reached for her wrist, felt no pulse. Even less was his inclination to feel her neck, but he did. Still, there was no pulse. He looked closer at her face, kneeling over her as Michael had done earlier. The woman was dead all right. And yes, she was beautiful, or at least she had been. Leonard noticed that the woman appeared to be older than he at first thought. Older than what Michael appeared to be. He guessed Michael to be about twenty-six, maybe twenty-seven, twenty-eight tops. This woman was in her mid to late forties, maybe even older. She was petite, and very well taken care of. Only up close did he notice the creases in her face. A tuck here, a tuck there, hell, maybe she hadn't even needed plastic surgery. Her body was in great shape. Well, aside from the fact that she was dead, she was in great shape. Leonard eased away, the back of his left hand grazing her thigh, just below where her skirt rode up beneath her. An electric chill danced up his spine. A tingle of excitement swelled up within him, tantalizing. He backed quickly up and away from her. A bit of cigarette ash tumbling to her leg and then rolling to the carpet between her legs, just at her shin. Leonard gazed at her long shapely legs again as he eased up, using the arm of the chair for support as he rose. He was out of breath, being a little overweight didn't help. I need to get in shape, he thought. He started to chuckle at the thought. How many times in the last ten of his own forty years had he said that? He sat on the edge of the chair and picked up his drink again, finishing it off. He glanced at the drink he had brought for Michael, but didn't pick it up, not yet. The woman's leg caught his attention again.

He noticed the ankle bracelet. She certainly dressed a lot younger than she should have, but she did have the body for it. His eyes slid up her and to the edge of her upturned skirt. He glanced quickly at her face, as though double checking again, just to make sure she was dead. He listened for Michael, but there wasn't any sound coming from the hallway. He should probably go check on him. In a minute. He looked around the room and almost started humming to himself as he took another quick glance at the woman's face then reached out and picked up the edge of her skirt. He held it up for a brief second or two before letting it drop again. A chill went up his spine. This is sick, he thought. I'm losing it. It was only then that he saw Michael come around the corner from the hallway. He jumped nervously up to his feet, and his cigarette fell to the carpet. He snatched it up and shoved it back into his mouth, hastily turning away from Michael, moving over to the cabinet.

Leonard cleared his throat and asked, "so, you okay?" He picked up the framed picture of the woman, then set it nervously back down.

"I guess."

Leonard wasn't sure whether Michael had seen him or not. Michael's voice was calm and even. He seemed okay, like everything was cool. Maybe he hadn't seen him. Maybe he had just walked into the room a second after. Something wasn't right though, something weird. He had only looked at Michael for a brief second as the kid had returned to the room, but—He turned and looked at Michael. He knew something wasn't right. He turned slowly. "Your scotch is on the table," he said absently. He looked at Michael full on, taking him in completely with his eyes, the full view. He had seen it when Michael had first entered, but it hadn't registered through his own embarrassment; the mascara, the rouge, the fake lashes, earrings dangling, even the bra and panties, black silk. He saw them now though. Yes sirree, now he had an eyeful. His mouth hung open in astonishment. The cigarette, now in his hand was burning all the way down to his knuckles, but he didn't seem to notice. He couldn't believe what he was seeing.

Michael gave Leonard a faint, seductive smile through pursed lips covered in a hot red lipstick. He blew Leonard a kiss and winked at him. He moved slowly toward Leonard, enticingly, ever confident in the role of seductress. Leonard stood still, too stunned to move, or to ward off Michael's advance. Michael was within inches, still smiling, moving ever so close before Leonard reacted. But react Leonard did. He was shaking, barely able to control his anger. A sheer seething anger it was, mixed with fear, an almost maniacal, spiraling fear. He lunged at Michael, wrenching the knife from Michael's hand and flinging him up against the wall. They knocked into the cabinet, sending the framed pictures and various other knick-knacks flying. A vase fell and broke against the edge of the cabinet, before cascading in pieces to the floor. Leonard had slammed Michael hard against the wall, knocking the wind out of him. A picture hanging on the wall was knocked loose, dangling; its framed corner wedged into Michael's neck, gouging him. Leonard leaned in close, the knife held firmly in his hand. He had Michael pinned against the wall, and was holding the knife to his throat. There appeared to be fear in Michael's eyes now. "You, sick fuck," Leonard seethed, breathing heavily. "I should kill you." The two just stared at one another. Someone banged on the wall from next door. Leonard loosened his grip a little on Michael, and pulled the knife back a fraction of an inch.

Michael puckered his lips and pretended to blow a soft kiss. Leonard tightened his grip on the knife and then stopped, catching himself. He threw the knife onto the floor and continued to hold Michael up against the wall. He had his forearm shoved against Michael's neck. He pressed firmly against

Michael's neck, cutting off his air. Michael gasped, then Leonard let up. The two men's eyes were glued to each other. Michael gave him a weak smile. Leonard spit into Michael's face in disgust and let him fall to the floor. He heaved a heavy sigh, then mumbled something about Michael being a pathetic bastard and left, slamming the door behind him.

Michael slumped against the wall, but remained in a sitting position on the floor. He took in some air and rubbed his neck gingerly. He smiled in the growing darkness of the apartment, then reached up with a handkerchief and collected the spittle from his face, careful to gather only a smidgen of makeup base with it. He would rather have not gotten any of the makeup with it, but it couldn't be helped. It didn't matter. The woman wore the same kind. He bent over the body and rubbed a bit of the spittle on the woman's lips, just at the corner. Then he lifted her skirt, just as Leonard had done earlier, and strategically placed more of it. It wouldn't much matter, sperm or saliva. Each contained the same telling signs, the same DNA structure. Next Michael lifted the woman's arm and wrapped her fingers around the one glass of remaining scotch, pressing firmly . . .

Incontrovertible Evidence

***

"Fasten your seatbelt Hon," the flight attendant said. "We'll be taking off any second now. Would you like me to stow that for you?"

"No thanks," Michael responded pushing the small bag up under the seat in front of him. He smiled at the thought of the thousands of dollars stuffed inside. He was also comforted by the thought of having securely wired the rest of the half a million dollars to his Swiss account. The flight attendant smiled back and proceeded up the aisle to settle into her own seat for takeoff. The engines whirred and whined as the jet climbed into the night sky. After the captain's greeting, and the leveling off of the plane, Michael eased his seatback down a little and settled in dreamily. He couldn't keep the thought of Leonard from creeping into his mind. The look on Leonard's face when he saw Michael in drag was just too much. The bra and panties worked perfectly. Leonard was stunned. So stunned, in fact that he hadn't even noticed the long black gloves that Michael had worn, even though they rose elegantly all the way up his forearms. Hell, Leonard hadn't even noticed the knife right off. The knife. Things could have ended badly with that, if nothing but by pure accident. Fortunately for Michael they hadn't. He would have to work out something different next time. He couldn't take the chance of getting stabbed. Well, anyway, the knife was only secondary. The woman had been strangled, not stabbed. It was meant merely to punctuate the whole scene. Leonard's fingerprints would be on it, of course, showing that he had meant to use it, that he was a man with violent intent. His fingerprints would also be on the glasses and the bottle of scotch, and God only knows what else he had touched while Michael had been in the bathroom. The fingerprints would only be a part of the whole composite though. What else would help with the conviction, would be the other scrapings and droppings and bits and pieces that had been painstakingly gathered by Michael over the past eight months.

It had been a godsend that Leonard had gotten so drunk that he had dropped his keys and then conveniently passed out in the car long enough for Michael to have a complete set made at the local Kmart on the way home from the bar. Modern convenience. After that it had been a cinch for Michael to simply slip into Leonard's house at will and collect the things he needed. Bits of hair and skin from

Incontrovertible Evidence

Leonard's hairbrush and his razor, nail clippings, threads, etc. Hell, Leonard could have lived at the woman's apartment for six months and not left half as much evidence as Michael had planted. A little hair on the pillow, a little bit of skin under the dead woman's fingernails, and of course, the saliva, actual secretion of bodily fluid from the murderer. What more could one ask for?

What of Leonard's story? Would he be believed? Honestly? Probably not. If he repeated what Michael had told him about the woman being his ex-wife and that he had told her he would kill her if he saw her again. Well that was just a sob story for Leonard to believe so he could help his friend out of the predicament. "I just happen to say I'm going to kill her, and then she just happens to turn up dead." Well, there is no way to tie Michael to the woman because she wasn't his ex-wife. She had been married, oh yes, most definitely, and to a very wealthy man. A lot of stocks, that sort of thing. That's what he had left her when he passed on about a year and a half before the woman got herself, Mrs. Elinore Dunstowe, murdered by her supposed lover, a Mr. Leonard Richardson.

Katherine Palmeri. She would be the only connection to Michael—"Would you care for a drink, hon ?"

Michael rubbed his eyes and stretched ever so languidly, and as delicately as he dared. "Just an orange juice please."

Amenities attended to, Michael settled back once again and drifted into thought. Katherine Palmeri, yes, she would be the only connection. She was the one who rented an apartment in the same building as Elinore Dunstowe, though not too close, not even on the same floor. She had moved into the building shortly after Mr. Dunstowe had passed away. One might even say she had followed Elinore there. Being that they were both new tenants, they got along quite well. Elinore wanted to maintain a low profile before deciding what to do next with her life and her money. Katherine became quite a friend to Elinore, a confidante. Katherine was younger, and helped Elinore with her wardrobe selection; and was helping to prepare her for dating again. She even offered to introduce her to her twin brother, Michael. After all, Elinore was still quite young and attractive. Elinore never met Michael though--well, not formally. Katherine advised Elinore in many things. She was actually amazed at the sheltered life the woman had led. They had become quite good friends in the very short span of just a couple of months. They played tennis together. They shopped together. They had even planned a trip to Europe together. Well, not just Europe. They planned to circle the globe, to jet set a little. The trip would be financed, of course, by the half a million dollars in stock that Elinore would sell. There was much more. Half a million seemed reasonable enough. No need to be greedy. Elinore converted the stock shares to cash just a day or so before she was so brutally murdered. A pity.

And what of this Katherine Palmeri, this connection? Was she a suspect? Could she even be found? The last time anyone had seen her was when the doorman had held the door for her and helped her load her bags into the waiting taxi. She had mentioned that her sister in San Francisco had taken ill rather suddenly, and she was going to take care of her. Miss Palmeri had asked the doorman to make sure her friend, Elinore, received the note she had given him explaining that they would have to postpone the trip to Europe until further notice. She said that she had knocked on Elinore's door but had received no answer. "Would he be so kind as to give Elinore the note upon Elinore's return?" she asked.

She left no address where she could be reached in San Francisco, and yet she sent money every month to cover her rent. After about six months she sent word that her sister had passed on. and she, Miss Katherine Palmeri would not be returning. She made arrangements by mail that her things be transferred to storage and that's the last anyone ever heard of her. Later on, had anyone bothered to check, they would have found the belongings auctioned off as abandoned.

And what of Michael, himself? Leonard had been the only one who had known him. There was no real address listed in the personnel file for Michael Greene, and no one even knew if it was the same person, or even what Michael Greene did for the company. The description given out seemed vaguely familiar, but no one could give anything definite to back up Leonard's story. Leonard didn't have a lot of friends. Oh sure, everyone knew who he was though. Everyone was appalled at what he had done to that poor woman.

And what of Leonard? Well, of course he was convicted. The evidence was sufficient enough. One might even say it was incontrovertible. A couple of suits of clothing belonging to him were found in her

Incontrovertible Evidence

closet, a pair of his shoes under her bed; his toothbrush in her bathroom. Soiled underwear and socks which had been worn by him were found in a clothes basket along with the deceased's clothes. And what about the love letters he had sent. All of this proves that he, in fact, knew and had relations with the woman in spite of all his protestations.

Not to mention all of the other, more convincing and incriminating evidence, such as the skin under her fingernails, the tiny bit of nail they found that had scraped her cheek and fallen into her hair as he strangled her and she fell to the floor. And there was the doorman from the woman's building who had made a postive ID. Yes, Leonard had been the man who had left the building that evening in an angry and highly disturbed state. It was about an hour or so before Miss Palmeri had left to visit her sick sister. How he had gotten in no one was quite sure; But it didn't seem to matter, what with all the other evidence.

"Put your seat up hon' we'll be landing in a couple of minutes."

Michael smiled.

Michael thought again of the look on Leonard's face and just shook his head. He thought about it as

Mark Stattelman

he, Michael, a.k.a Katherine Palmeri, or rather more recently, as the plane ticket read, Janet Anderson, waited at the baggage carousel. And again, he thought of it before he left the hotel room. A room he had rented under the name of Jack L. Cartier. He glanced in the mirror before leaving the room and had to laugh. He straightened his tie and picked a piece of lint from his evening jacket, then took his ivory tipped walking stick in hand. Jack was a little more of girth than Michael, a little older, and yes, a little more dignified. Who couldn't be more dignified with half a million in cash neatly tucked away in a Swiss account? Oh well, there was more than that, from previous jobs. It wasn't really the money after all, though, but the joys of the occupation; the art of it all. He felt a little sad at times, whenever he thought about Leonard and some of the others. Maybe he was beginning to go soft? Maybe he should think about retiring? Ah, he'd give it some thought, later. Much later, he thought as he watched the French beauty walking toward him down the hall. He always loved the Riviera. He stopped and watched her pass. She smiled at him just before disappearing around the corner. He smiled inwardly with a self-satisfied glow, then moved on down the hall. Where was he? Oh yes, ruminating about Leonard again. He decided that the only thing Leonard and those like him had done was to be in the wrong place at the wrong time; and yes, the fact that they befriended him didn't help their situation. He sighed. Someone had to take the fall, that was the sad part. If only he could find a way around that. Ah, but that wouldn't work. It would be an incomplete job if someone didn't get caught. Justice had to prevail. Always. There was no way around it. He would just have to be more particular about the friends he picked. Maybe he could pick less likeable people? But that would make the job so much more disagreeable. And the people would sense his dislike. There was no way he could hide such a thing. They, of course, would be less inclined to cooperate if they sensed his dislike for them. It wouldn't work. At least not in practice. He decided that it was a treacherous thing to befriend him though. Often times extremely treacherous. How often had men gone to the gallows for him? Hmm, far too often to think about. Guilt by association. Ha. But then what are friends for--If not for framing? And he did it so nicely too, so picture perfect. Yet still he had to sigh at the thought of friendship. It simply wouldn't do for him to pat himself on the back too often, nor become too haughty. Humility was the key to friendship--At least according to Jack L. Cartier, one of the richest men on the Riviera, yet also one of the most humble. Yes, Jack was quite a guy, a real jewel of a man. Jack could be the perfect friend for just the right person.

A Gem, A Jewel. . . . Yes indeed, Jewels. And there was a certain lady that Jack was beginning to develop a fondness for lately. He knew this because he and Jack had grown quite close, quite close indeed, their thoughts sort of melding together. One might even say they were becoming one with each other. There was evidence of this, yes, a certain, eventual, incontrovertible evidence. He had grown extremely fond of Jack, very comfortable wearing Jack's clothes, walking in Jack's shoes. He might even, he decided, retire as Jack; Oh, not anytime soon, of course. There was plenty of money, yes, but it wasn't about that. It was, after all, about the art. One had to be quite careful with evidence. There couldn't be too much of it. He hesitated for a minute, thinking. Perhaps he had dumped too much onto Leonard? Hmm, maybe. He would have to lighten his touch next time, remain humble. No, one shouldn't try and be too clever. The evidence needed to be just enough. Just enough to sway a jury, enough to convict; Just enough to be incontrovertible.

NIGHT TRAIN

WE KNOW. That's what the note read; those two simple words. It was enough to strike terror into my heart. My head throbbed. My stomach churned. I am an old man now. How could I move again? I couldn't just pick up and leave, not again. I guess, well, perhaps . . . I would have to. I would do what was necessary. I had no choice.

***

The first time came back to me. Sixty years ago. The note. Those words: WE KNOW. I remember it too well. The man. "We will not hurt you," he had said. "It is only them we want, the Jews." He almost spewed the word, like bile. "The filthy Jews."

"But --" I protested.

"No. We will get them. With or without your help." He crumpled the newspaper he had been speaking from behind. His face was narrow, coming to almost a point at the chin. There was a small white scar, just a small half-moon shape on his chin. His hair line was receding, graying at the temples. Leaning in close, he looked at me. His eyebrows rose and came together. His blue- gray eyes were hard and cold, yet full of passion, a fiery anger. He sat in a heated silence, simmering. The paper was wet now, soaking up the grease from his plate. His cigarette burned in the ashtray.

Did he know about me? I wondered. Did he know that I was Jewish on my mother's side? I guessed not. His tone would have been different. He probably would not have been speaking to me at all. In the end it wouldn't have mattered.

"Everything all right, sir?" The steward asked. Looking at him from a dark face, a pearl smile, the whites of his eyes glistening.

"Yes," The man smiled, his countenance changing completely.

Night Train

After the steward left, he looked at me for a second over the rim of his coffee cup. His hand was steady as he brought the cup down. "Just remember what I said." And he was gone. The remains of his cigarette burned in the ashtray. His coffee cup rattled in the saucer, swirling the remnants of the brown liquid as the train jolted and jostled steadily along the tracks. I looked out the window. The landscape was a blur of snowy, open country. America, I thought. Even here. They had followed.

The plan had been simple. We were to leave the compartment doors open that night. My wife was staying in the same compartment with my employer's wife. And I was in the same compartment with my employer, The Jew. Yes, it was easier that way. The men together, and the women in the other compartment along with the children. I had explained it to my wife. We had no choice. We would do as asked. "But how do you know they will not also kill us?" She asked.

"I don't know. We have to take them at their word."

"Their word, huh! You trust that?"

"No, but we have no choice."

"I will tell her."

"You can't. You must not."

"But this is America," she said. "They can't get away with it. We are free now. We can go to the authorities."

"There isn't time. Besides, they will not believe us. We have no proof, nothing." I was gripping her by the shoulders, my thumbs making indentations. She looked at me, her large dark eyes moist with fear. I hadn't realized how tightly I held her.

"You're hurting me." Her lips were compressed, fear turning to anger. I could see the pain in her eyes. A lump was in my throat. In our almost two years of marriage I had never handled her this way.

Someone was coming down the narrow passageway toward us, strangers. They eyed us suspiciously for a moment. I gave a weak smile, and a nod. They entered a compartment close by.

"I will not give in to them," she said. "I will not leave the door unlocked."

"Okay." I said. "Okay. Just don't tell. They have been through enough. Perhaps I'll think of something, some way out. . ."

She looked at me as I let go. I had tried to kiss her, just a quick peck on the cheek, but she turned away.

Night Train

I watched her move down the short passage to her compartment. I wished we could have gotten side by side arrangements, but we couldn't. We had been too late. She glanced back over her shoulder once more, her eyes uncertain yet imploring. Then her thick dark hair, and the folds of her dress were all I saw as she went inside. I yearned for her, and for some way out. I stood in the passage and thought as the train jolted. Nothing came to me. Darkness approached. I went into my own compartment to face my employer.

He looked up and smiled as I entered. His eyes were small and searching, peering at me over gold rimmed glasses. His smile was genuine. He put away the pen and closed the book he had been writing in, wrapping the ribbon back around it and binding it tightly. "Trouble, Joseph?" He asked, folding his glasses and slipping them into his pocket.

"Hm?" Then I realized he meant marriage trouble. He could always tell. "No sir," I said. He knew I was lying. He was like a kindly old father. He always knew. Better he not know the truth, though; Not yet. Perhaps I would tell him. He had been through worse. Now he was relaxed though, happy to be free.

I would not spoil it. Not now. They would come. Of course, they would come. Should I let him die happily? They would get him anyway, just as they had gotten his children. An unfortunate accident. Eventually they would win.

He smiled that knowing smile and I could read his thoughts: You'll tell me in your own good time! And he would have been right, normally. He looked out the window at the wide expanse rolling rhythmically past. The sun was almost completely down now. The flat skyline was punctuated by snowy fields, with dark, sporadic shadows of trees springing up over and over. "I can smell it," he said.

"What's that, sir?" I asked, knowing full well what he meant. He had not truly relaxed even when the ship reached New York. It was only on this train, now, Chicago bound, that he was beginning to feel freedom, a new life. I did not need to remind him that he was a German physicist, a Jew, that the Nazis would never let live to see a new life in a new land. Let him dream.

We sat in silence for a few seconds and then he heaved a sigh. Perhaps thinking of his lost family, his children. He glanced at his pocket watch in the fading light and then shoved it back into his pocket.

Night Train

He stood and worked the bed down from the bulkhead. "Shouldn't we wait on the porter?" I asked.

"No need." Then he paused. "Perhaps you can find us a nightcap."

It was then that it hit me. Of course, I would.

I was out of the compartment and practically at a run to locate what I needed. Sleeping powders weren't that difficult to come by, and it was just as easily slipped into his glass of water. He always liked to refer to it as a "nightcap" for some reason, just a habit he had picked up somewhere. I sat in fear, hoping he wouldn't taste the powder in the water. He looked strangely at the glass after taking the first sip, but didn't say anything. I was determined he wouldn't see them coming for him. And then I worked up a plan of my own.

It was a restless twenty minutes or so before I finally heard his breathing grow to a steady rhythm. And then I set to work. I searched in vain until finally spotting his partially open satchel. It was old and there was a loop of strong wire that he used to bind it shut. The wire was passed through holes on the top of the satchel, and then on each end of the wire were eye holes formed to be locked together with a small padlock. The lock was still undone. He usually locked it, but tonight he had merely dropped his small book within, and forgotten. It took a few minutes, but I was able to work the wire loose from the holes and the satchel. Breathing heavily, I waited. The only sound was Jacob's breathing, and the steady rhythm of the moving train. I waited patiently, but nothing happened for a long time. The rhythm of the train began to work on me. Mentally, I became fraught. I stood in the darkness, picturing the man's face in my mind, his eyebrows lurching upwards at me as he peered across the breakfast table in the dining car. I could hear the rattle of his cup against the saucer. I could see his blue-gray eyes glaring at me, threatening. We Know, his note had said. When he slid into the seat across from me his words were a sibilant threat, "We know you are traveling with the Jew, helping him elude us . . ." I waited, hearing only the moving train, seeing only the man's face in the darkness. I realized I was holding my breath. I let it out slowly, trying to relax. Then I waited again, nothing but the darkness, and the rhythm of the moving train, then the man's face again. I thought I heard the compartment door open; I could almost see it start to slide open. It was only my imagination, nothing, only darkness, and

Night Train

the moving train. I listened for Jacob's breathing, forgetting again my own. Silence. Darkness. My nerves tightening again till I was like a coiled spring, ready to pounce. The train jolted and someone fell against the bulkhead outside in the passage. I wanted to run screaming from the compartment. Silence again. Only the rhythmic rattling of the train as it moved down the track filled the night air. Then the door opened and I lunged. I pulled the wire tight, and tighter still around the throat of my prey. The body crumpled to the compartment floor. I heard the jangle of keys. The porter. My God.

I grabbed the keys and ran from the compartment. I had to find my wife. I had to do something. I ran to her door. It was not locked. Oh, God no. I pushed it open and fell into someone in the tight compartment. There was a loud "umph" as we fell together. I could feel hot breath on my neck. A jumble of hair, the smell of perfume, a coat, a luger. I pulled the trigger and the body went limp beneath me. Somehow, I knew it wasn't my wife, nor Jacob's wife. She would have been too old, too fragile. This one was strong, agile. I turned her over and felt her face, the slickness. In the dim light of the half open door I could see the blood on my hands. I could feel the stickiness. I then saw my wife, the bullet hole in her temple. I lost my air, only a whimper escaped my lips. My feet failed me and I fell upon her, holding her. She was limp, slack in my arms. "Sophie," I cried. "Dear God, No!" I trembled with grief. My trembling stopped almost as soon as it began when I distinguished a whimpering cry in the darkness. It was then that I realized I was lying across Jacob's wife. It wasn't her who cried though, for she also had been shot dead. The cry was my baby daughter, Marie. She lay next to my wife, under a pillow. I lifted the pillow and held her in my arms. Apparently, I had interrupted the assassin as she was attempting to smother my baby girl. So that would explain the luger not being at the ready when I barreled through the door. Oh, God. My darling . . . My beautiful baby girl. Oh, Marie, Oh Sophie, Oh. Oh. Dear God. Oh Jacob. The man, where was the man. I sprang up, the baby in my arms, falling again to my knees as I tripped over the Nazi assassin. I started again, stumbling out the door, holding the baby, the luger. A woman screamed in the passageway. I moved past her and then turned and thrust my Marie into her arms. I had to pull her arms and hands down from her screaming mouth and force

Night Train

the baby into them. There was the man. He had exited the car with Jacob slung drowsily across his shoulder. He was going to throw him overboard, an accident, yes. I lunged for his coat tails and missed. He turned to fire. I fired first, wildly, the bullet ripping through his cheek like an upper cut, from the bottom of his jaw upward. He toppled backwards, his arms flying up and out, Jacob's added weight pushing him over, toppling him, I lunged forward, but the moving train jerked spasmodically pushing me even further in my forward movement, while the closing door caught my foot. It ripped my shoe off and twisted my leg. And I was thrown from the train to the rocky, snowy bank below. From there I watched the train speeding away into the night, carrying with it my dead wife and my baby girl. The vision was only momentary. Silence followed as I lay and looked up from the snow bank into the full pale moon. The stars twinkled brightly, and I could see my breath rising upward. That was all I knew until I passed out, and then woke up hours later as I was being pulled by sled to a nearby farm house. From there I was transported to another home, further away. The home of a Jewish doctor. I was in great pain, but I survived. The man and Jacob had both been killed in the fall from the train. Perhaps the man had been dead beforehand due to the bullet. I was lucky. But I didn't feel lucky. They had succeeded. They had killed the Jew physicist.

I couldn't help thinking that perhaps I could have thrown my daughter into the snowy embankment, and that, somehow, she would have survived the fall. Perhaps, if I had not been in a fight with the man. It might have been possible. Just maybe. I almost drove myself crazy thinking about it. I watched the newspapers for any news. There was a lot of coverage for about a week or two. I listened intently to the radio. The war was on full swing then. A few individual deaths on a night train could not hold anyone's attention for long. I was truly sorry for the porter. I had not intended to kill him. I wasn't sure I had actually intended to kill anyone. One is often times forced into desperate acts by circumstance. This I have come to believe. This is how I justify it.

So the woman in the passage gave my description to the police. I was the murderer for all anyone knew. I was the bad guy. Through connections, I was eventually helped to get a new identity. A job. I moved around. I searched orphanage after orphanage for my daughter. It was again through Jewish connections that I found her five years later. A nice couple adopted her. After another year or so I left with her in the middle of the night. We settled in Arizona. I eventually married again to a wonderful woman. I worked for thirty years with an accounting firm. My daughter grew up happily and had a couple of brothers along the way. She never knew the story. My new wife never knew. No one.

My wife died a couple of years ago in her sleep. I miss her. I also miss Sophie terribly. Sometimes I wake up in the middle of the night in a cold sweat, the man's face before me. "We know . . ." He starts his accusation. I see his scar, his chin. I hear the rattle of his cup and saucer. It is usually a couple of seconds before I see the rest, the bullet ripping into his jaw, his tumbling from the train to meet death. Who was the woman assassin? How many more were there? Will they still be looking for me? There are more of them out there, a faction of them. Do they have my picture in a file somewhere? Will they send someone after me? Will they find me?

***

WE KNOW, the note reads. I flip it over and continue, my heart stopping.

Mark Stattelman

THAT IT'S YOUR BIRTHDAY BECAUSE A LITTLE BIRDIE TOLD US!

  They all burst in through the office door singing "For he's a jolly good fellow . . ." I am stunned. "Happy eightieth!" I hear. "Happy Birthday, Karl." Voices all gather round me. "Mr. Schmidt." And again. "Happy Birthday, Grandpa!".

  The words are still echoing in my head, WE KNOW. But they don't know. They can never know.

  "Susie, get grandpa a glass of water," I hear. "He looks pale." "Are you okay Karl?" Another voice echoes.

  "Dad?"

  Marie looks at me, but it is Sophie's eyes I see as she disappears into the compartment. And I hear the train rumbling along the track, a lifetime ago, disappearing into the night.

CLACKERS

"**D**anny Parkiese died," my wife said, putting down her pocketbook and coming over to where I sat at the dining room table. She pronounced it like Park-easy. I didn't bother to tell her it was pronounced more like Park-ee-ezzee. She wasn't from around here and hadn't really known any of them. It didn't much matter, I guessed, since he was dead anyway. "Val told me," she continued. I folded up the newspaper and laid it aside. I took a drink of my now lukewarm coffee. She had just come home from having her hair done. I had made a sandwich for lunch. It was our usual routine for a Wednesday. Well, my routine was pretty much the same every day since I had retired;

She always got her hair done on Wednesdays. "Wasn't he a friend of yours?"

I cleared my throat. I needed time to think about it. I shrugged and nodded. She hadn't been looking when I responded. She had started into the kitchen.

"Hmm?" She asked, sort of looking back over her shoulder at me.

"Yeah, I guess," I said.

"What did you have?"

"Ham and cheese on toast."

She frowned a little and moved on to the refrigerator, opening the door and rummaging about. "I'm gonna have some of the left-over chicken," she said. She opened the Tupperware container and brought it up to her face, sniffing it. It was something she always did. She got a plate and silverware out, setting it on the counter. She came over to retrieve my cup of coffee. "You 'guess'?" She picked up the mug and took it into the kitchen. She stuck it in the microwave and heated it.

"What?" I asked.

"I figured I'd heat your coffee before I stuck the chicken in . . ." There was a slight pause. The micro-

Clackers

wave dinged. "You guess?" She repeated. "Most people know if they are friends or not." She brought the coffee back over and set it on the table.

"Well, yeah. I just meant . . ."

"And you had that thing a few years back, and . . ."

"Yeah, it's just that I mostly knew him way back when we were kids." She had popped her chicken into the microwave and come back. She was standing there, looking at me, her hands on her hips. A couple of seconds went by. She shrugged and went back into the kitchen. She scurried around, got a glass out and then poured herself some ice tea from a pitcher. The microwave dinged and she pulled the chicken out. She stood slicing the chicken off of the bone and placing it on a couple slices of bread. I took a sip of my coffee and watched her dart around. I mainly saw her backside. The whole time I was thinking about Danny Parkiese and not even worrying about classifying him as a friend or not. When I thought about Danny, I thought mostly about clackers. He drove people crazy with them when we were in the fourth grade. You'd have to be pretty old to remember the toy; and I imagine even people who were old enough had probably forgotten them. Clackers were a toy that was really popular for a short while in the late sixties and early nineteen seventies. Then they just disappeared. Clackers got pulled off the shelves and outlawed, deemed unsafe. Supposedly, I guess, some exploded and tore up a kid's face, or knocked an eye out or something. All we had heard was that they were then outlawed. Who knows what actually happened? I do know that they had definitely been unsafe for Danny Parkiese, but in a totally different way. What they were, was—and you can look it up on YouTube and see the old commercials advertising them—two acrylic balls hanging from two ends of a cord, or two cords, I guess. One ball hanging on each outer end. There was a small ring in the middle, between the two cords, or sometimes a small piece of dowel or wood. The balls were a very hard acrylic, and were maybe an inch and a half in diameter. You would hold your arm out in front of you, holding the ring. You lifted your arm in an up and down motion to get the balls going and they would clack together and bounce off of each other, making a clacking sound. The motion would continue, and the clack would become rhythmic. Once the balls were set in motion, there would be very little effort required to keep them going. It

Clackers

was a fad. It was a fad that a few kids took to fervently. Danny was one of those kids. The toy was sometimes called something else, but I don't remember what the other name was. And the balls came in several colors. I remember a caramel colored set. I remembered them reflecting the sun as they bounced. Anyway, Danny had a habit of driving people crazy with them. He would come up behind the other kids, and holding the clackers close to the person's ear, start clacking away. He could be a real pest. He got me a couple of times. He really did piss some kid off, or maybe a couple of kids were behind what happened. But that's where I come into the picture. I was the one who found him. The balls were wrapped around his neck, the cord anyway, and he was unconscious. I found him, just lying there. I think he had been strung up on the hook on the back of the bathroom stall door. You gotta understand, Danny was a small kid back then. I think it was 1970 or '71. Anyway, they rushed him to the hospital and he lived. He changed schools after that. I don't think anyone ever found out who had done it. I don't think Danny ever told. Could have been due to fear. I don't know. In any case, he was gone. Gone from school, gone from my life. Though I don't remember being that close to him, we had hung out together briefly, before the clacker incident. I really just remember him swiping a couple of cigarettes out of his mom's purse one time, and a couple of beers out of the refrigerator. We sat in the woods that one day after school and hung out drinking and smoking. We were eleven or twelve, I believe, at the time. But it had to have been before the clacker incident, and it was a very short-lived friendship, if you can even call it that. Didn't see him, or even think about him for years after that.

"Mm," my wife said, taking a bite of her sandwich. She had sat down at the table across from me. "This is good," she said. "Want a bite?" I shook my head and took another sip of coffee. "Missing out," she said. I noticed she had also made a salad. She forked a bite into her mouth and then took a drink of tea.

"What did he die from?"

"Huh?"

"Danny."

"Oh, yeah," she had taken another bite and I had to wait a second or two on her answer. She sort of brought her hand up to cover her mouth. "Val didn't say. I don't think she knew. You know Val. She tells it all, so if she had known she would have spilled it."

Clackers

I nodded.

"Thinking of going to the funeral?"

"I dunno. You just did spring it on me. Hadn't really had time to give it any thought." "Probably not," I said after a long pause.

She shrugged and continued eating. We sat silent for a few more minutes. I got busy with other things that afternoon and didn't really think about Danny Parkiese the rest of the day.

That night was a different story. I closed my eyes and his whole family paraded around in front of me. I remembered his sister, Janet and could see her clearly. She was a year older than us. I remember having a little bit of a crush on her for a short time, but she was older and didn't even notice. I think she left right after high school. Last I heard, she had gone to California. I think everyone lost track of her after that, including her family. Danny's older brother, two years older than us, ended up at Riker's and then I believe he got shivved for some reason by another inmate, and died. Mr. Parkiese worked at the mill, same as my father. I believe he died of cancer when we were in high school. The mother, well, she was the last one living. She died a few years back; cirrhosis of the liver. Danny had been the last one left, at least around here. I think maybe there had been some cousins a couple of towns over.

There was something that happened a few years back, however, regarding Danny. And that was what my wife had referred to at lunch. I was still on the police force then, a detective. Danny had been hit by a car while crossing the street. He had been in a coma. No one knew if he would make it, and only he knew who the driver had been. I believe his mother was still alive then. She wasn't in the best of shape at that time.

Anyway, I had had problems of my own. There is a disease, a brain disorder, and I was firmly convinced I suffered from it. I had read about it somewhere, and I can't remember what it was called. But it was where someone, the person suffering from it, no longer sees things linearly. In other words, the person just sees things in snapshots. They can't do things like pour a glass of juice, or whatever. It is like a string of film, with frames missing. As the person pours the juice into a glass, the missing frames might be when the glass becomes full. So the person sees the glass almost full, and then the next picture they get is the liquid spilling out onto the table. Needless to say, this makes things difficult. Even

Clackers

crossing the street is dangerous for the person suffering this disease. The CAT scan showed nothing, of course. And after a series of other tests, the doctor told me there was nothing wrong. But, all the same, I was having the same problems as someone with that disease. The doctor sent me to a "specialist," who was really just a psychologist, I believe. Here's the thing: The symptoms just started, right out of the blue. These symptoms started at the time Danny Parkiese was in a coma. And, to make it all even more weird, I could hear the sound of clackers. The sound of the balls clacking together changed the picture in my mind. It was like the clicking of a shutter on a camera and then flashes. These flashes would be things from the past, present, and get this, even from or of the future. I never mentioned the future part of things to either of the doctors. But it was there too, just like the present and past. The present was probably the hardest to deal with. It was difficult to function. I tried as best I could. And then things just got even more weird. Perhaps it was due to the sound of clackers that brought Danny to mind. I went to the hospital to see him. I hadn't seen him since we had been kids. I hadn't seen him since that day I had found him in the bathroom stall. No, of course, that isn't true. I had seen him a couple of days after that. For some reason, the authorities had not taken the clackers. I had picked the clackers up off the bathroom floor. I had unwrapped the cord from Danny's neck, of course. And when the medical folks got there, they were more interested in getting Danny to the hospital than they were about the toy. I stood holding the clackers. Things were a lot different then. The adults just saw me as the kid who found Danny. No big investigation, nothing. So there I stood. I had picked the clackers up from the floor and stood there holding them by my side. I started to hold them out at one point, but then backed out of the way to let the stretcher pass by. No one asked for the clackers after that. I think the principal started to, but then a concerned teacher asked him a question, and he got sidetracked. There had been a lot of commotion then. It had been a big deal. And then, when I got questioned later, I had just said I found him on the floor. For some reason, I didn't mention the clackers. When Danny got out of the hospital a few days later, I rode over to his house on my bike and gave the clackers to him. I wasn't sure he was gonna want them after what had happened; but then I knew he

Clackers

had been really attached to them. When I held the clackers out to him that day as we stood there on his front porch, he just looked at me a second, and then he reached out and took them. I had asked him if he wanted them and he hesitantly nodded yes. I had asked how he was doing, just prior to this, and he said okay. I had asked him if he was gonna be coming to school the next day and he just shrugged. Then he didn't. He never returned. His older sister was there still, and his brother. But not Danny. I didn't see him for years after that. It wasn't until he had suffered the hit and run, when he was in the coma. Not until I was seeing pictures in my head that flashed forward to the sound of clackers. There would sometimes be the bright flash of light, just before the vision appeared. The light was there more often when the vision would be of the future.

***

And so, it was the year 2000. And there I stood, looking down at Danny as he lay there with tubes coming out of him. He had changed, of course. He looked nothing like he had as a twelve-year old child. Perhaps if his eyes had been open there might have been something that made him the same. But no, he wasn't the same. Nor was I. I remember standing there and hearing the sound of the respirator. And there was another sound, the sound of the clackers. It rose up, that sound. I could distinctly hear the two balls smacking into one another, clacking. And with each clack, came the pictures. I distinctly saw Danny being hit. I saw him flying up onto the hood of a vehicle. I saw it from the outside, and then through Danny's eyes. It was in slow motion. He would be suspended in the air, then with the next click, the next picture, he would be in a different position. And as Danny was suspended there in the air, looking through his eyes, I could see clearly. I could see old man Withers behind the wheel of his red pickup truck. I knew who had hit Danny and taken off. Withers had been drunk, heavily intoxicated. And Withers had panicked and driven off as quickly as he could after hitting Danny. No one had been around. It was only afterward that Mrs. Vance, a concerned citizen, had driven by and seen Danny laying there in the road. Mrs. Vance had called 911.

  It had only been a matter of going to see Withers after that, and picking him up. He confessed. And his truck's headlight was busted. The trouble I had

Clackers

was making it look like there was a logical connection, a trail of evidence that made me suspect Withers. I wasn't even the detective on the case at the time. Fairfield was the detective. I knew him, but not well enough to explain things. I didn't know anyone that well.

Withers had confessed. He broke easily. He only looked puzzled when detective Fairfield mentioned that I had seen him driving around with a busted headlight and had brought the detective's attention to the possibility that he had been the one who had hit Danny Parkiese and taken off. Fortunately, Withers' guilty conscience had overridden his puzzlement and he folded. I don't know. Perhaps Withers had thought maybe there had been some sort of coincidence of another, similar truck, with a broken headlight. He had, I assumed, kept his truck hidden in the garage. He didn't know how we figured it out, but he knew he was guilty—that had been enough for him to crumble.

No, that case had been easy. It was the cases after that that had been difficult. Every time, it would be the sound of clackers, and the photos, or visions, that helped me solve the case. I would then have to figure out how I could explain. I would, in some cases, have to plant evidence, or rather, breadcrumbs leading to the evidence. I hated like hell doing it. But the evidence was always there. And that evidence was always overwhelming. The person was always guilty, in every case. My conscience was always clear on that point. I ended up having the biggest success rate in the whole state before I retired. My closed, or solved, cases far outnumbered everyone else's. No one could understand it. And I certainly couldn't. My only connection was the sound of the clackers and the visions that would come. I don't know whether it had anything to do with me helping Danny that day in school, the day I found him practically strangled in the stall. And none of it started until Danny had suffered the hit and run, and was in the coma. I have no idea what the connection was, but there was one.

Danny came out of the coma, of course, and I wasn't anywhere around when he came to. Detective Fairfield hurried over and explained to him that Withers had been arrested. I don't think my name ever even came up in the conversation.

***

Two weeks to the day my wife told me that Danny Parkiese had died, there was a FedEx delivery. I

Clackers

signed for the small box. My wife was having her hair done. I had answered the door. I didn't even have to open the box to know what was inside of it. The return address was to a law office in town. It was from the lawyer handling Danny's estate. I did open the box. I stood staring down into the box at the clackers. The sound of them clacking together filled my ears, my head. I saw flashes of light. But the light I then saw was the sunlight sparkling, and reflecting off the balls as they clacked together and then bounced apart. I was eleven years old again. Danny stood before me, grinning, moving his arm up and down. There were kids playing four square a short distance away. There was the sound of other kids playing and laughing. Then, the vision changed. I heard the sound of the balls hitting one another, same as always, and pictures rose up, different pictures. There was someone in a suit walking up to a small house in a town somewhere in sunny California. I knew that there was going to be a problem, however. I somehow knew that the man approaching the front door of the house would be given the news that Danny's sister had passed away a week before Danny had. She was much older in the vision that I now saw of her, no longer the school girl I had remembered. She had, at least according to the visions, been heavily intoxicated when she passed away. She might have died of cirrhosis of the liver eventually, just as Mrs. Parkiese had done. But no, Danny's sister had stumbled on the front step and fallen, hitting her head on the edge of the step.

I have no answers. I can't explain the connection, or why I can see these things. I could probably explain my hearing the sound of the clackers, as Danny was a maniac with them when we were kids. He drove us all crazy with them. I heard my wife come in the front door, home from having her hair done. At this point, I was out in the garage. I tucked the box with the clackers in it onto a shelf. I doubted I would ever open it again. I started into the house to meet my wife. The garage door had been closed. She had parked in the driveway. And she had walked up and into the front door as usual. Just as I started to climb the two steps leading from the garage into the house, I had two thoughts: 1)I hoped that I wasn't going to get a notice that Danny had left the house and all the rest of his belongings to me in case of his sister's death. And 2) The vision of

Clackers

Danny's skeleton rising up out of the grave, grinning, holding clackers and raising his arm in an up and down motion, clacking the balls together. I would have laughed at the vision, but couldn't. It terrified me. As I stepped into the kitchen, my wife turned to look at me. She had a weird, questioning look on her face. "What's up?" she asked. I didn't tell her.

COBRA'S DEMISE

(Think A.E.W. Mason's Hanaud (the original), rather than Agatha Christie's Poirot, with regard to the French detective. Or perhaps the detective in this story floats somewhere between the two.)

No one understood Carlyle better than Carlyle himself, but not even Carlyle could fully comprehend, much less even begin to appreciate the predicament he now found himself in. Not that anyone could appreciate such a predicament. He sat staring out of the train window, watching the shapes move past. He noticed his own reflection staring back at him in the glass, tousled sandy hair, a sullen, remote expression on his face, darkened circles round his eyes, a puffiness arising from only fitful snatches of restless sleep. He had just returned from India to London, found the letter, and had to leave home once again to journey to France, a much shorter trip albeit, but one he felt was very unnecessary. The whole thing seemed extremely absurd. The letter of warning was perplexing to say the least. Why on earth was Victor Bonaducce trying to kill him? And from the grave, no less?

He thought back to the last time he had seen Victor. It would have been over breakfast, three months prior, at Victor's villa. Who else would have been there? Anna. Yes, of course. Anna would have been. She was, in fact. And she had been lovelier than ever on that morning. Fresh as the French countryside on a spring day . . . Someone opened the door to Carlyle's compartment, interrupting his thoughts. "Sorry," came a voice. He caught only the momentary reflection in the glass of someone closing the compartment door again. By the time he turned his head they were gone. He looked back out the window. The countryside moved steadily past as the train continued on its rumbling way.

Where was he? Oh yes, Anna . . . He could still recall the scent of her as she leaned forward to whisper into his ear, her dark curls grazing his cheek. The sun was coming up over the edge of the house that morning, as he imagined it had done on many such mornings previous and since. It was slanting just enough into the window. Well, not quite enough, for that was why Anna had leaned over him to pull the curtains aside a little more, letting in more light along with more of the morning air. And that was when Victor yelled to close the "Bloody window." Anna had giggled and muttered something quickly into Carlyle's ear. He hadn't caught what she had said, because Victor had gone into his tirade, yelling about how everyone was hurrying his death along by opening blooming windows all over the house and suchlike. Victor had wheeled his chair around and caught his hand between the wheel on his chair and the edge of the table in the breakfast nook. This caused him to grow even more angry. By this point in his illness Victor had achieved a certain madness, sporadic episodes of purely psychotic raving punctuated by an inane calmness. Neither of these moods even remotely resembled his true character. Some of his behavior was the frustration of knowing the disease was getting the better of him. He had cancer, yes, but there seemed to be something more; for his total personality had changed, drastically, and for the worse.

Who else had been there that morning? Oh, Franz. Yes, Franz had just walked into the room at the end of the whole scene and--AHH-HA. . . Ah! To remain calm. Remain ever so calm. And not move, not a fraction of an inch. That would be the key. The Cobra sat staring at Carlyle, poised between his legs. How the snake had gotten into the compartment, Carlyle didn't know. He could venture to guess, yes. His money would have been on whoever had opened the compartment door only moments before. Only now did Carlyle spot the small cloth bag on the floor just inside the door. It lay limp and innocuous, while its deadly contents sat unwaveringly poised and ready to strike, only inches from Carlyle's left leg.

***

"I am trying to tell you, Inspector--Someone is attempting to KILL ME!"

"Yes, and the snake huh? The snake who just died of a . . . a 'heart attack' right between your very legs, just as he was about to strike, huh? He wants you dead too, no?"

"Pfh . . . Look--"

"A 'heart attack' you say," the inspector continued, leaning forward in his desk. "How do you know it was a heart attack? Are you a snake docteur, monsieur?" The diminutive inspector maintained a serious expression, but just barely. Having finished, he leaned back in his chair and tweaked his mustache.

"Look, I don't know if it was a heart attack or not." Carlyle's voice was rising in anger. He couldn't help it. "I don't even know if snakes have hearts for Godsakes! I just know someone is--"

"I know, I know--trying to kill you. You don't have to shout, monsieur. There is nothing wrong with my hearing."

Carlyle paced back and forth in the office of the local French prefect, raking his hands through his hair, and growing more frustrated with each passing moment.

The inspector let Carlyle stew for a minute or so before breaking silence. Finally, he said, "I think you are right monsieur."

Carlyle stopped pacing and eyed him. The inspector went on: "The snake must have had a heart. After all, he was on French soil. Everyone in France has a heart, no?" He grinned.

"Oh!" Carlyle threw his arms up in exasperation. "I bloody well wonder . . ." He started pacing again, then stopped. "You know, Inspector, I truly hope--"

There was a knock on the door to the inspector's office.

The inspector went out for a moment. Carlyle plopped onto the chair opposite the inspector's desk and placed his head in his hands. "How maddening," he muttered. "How positively bloody maddening." He hadn't mentioned the letter to the inspector. What was the point. The man would certainly

Cobra's Demise

think he had gone mad if he mentioned that a dead man was the one who was trying to kill him. Why shouldn't he be mad, though, after sharing a railway compartment with a cobra. Even after the snake died, he had sat transfixed, not sure that it was really dead. When he finally got up the gumption to move, his body almost couldn't be coaxed into moving. He had seen such snakes in India, but the ones he had observed had all been under the control of their masters, no more than harmless pets. This was different It all seemed like a very sick joke. The inspector soon returned. Someone entered the room behind him.

"This woman says she knows you, monsieur. She went to the station looking for you."

"Anna!" Carlyle jumped up, his heart leaping at the sight of her. There was a moment of awkwardness. Carlyle looked at the inspector, unsure whether he was free to leave.

"For now, you may leave, monsieur, but only under the . . ." he hesitated, searching for the proper word, "supervision of Madame Bonaducce. At least until we decide whether or not to arrest you--"

"Arrest me?" Carlyle was incredulous.

"Yes, monsieur, for bringing lethal snakes onto French soil."

Carlyle could not believe his ears. Anna tugged at his sleeve, pulling him towards the door. "I cannot help but wonder, monsieur . . ." the inspector continued. Carlyle stopped in his tracks, his mouth hanging open. Now what?

"Do you have the same effect on women that you have on snakes?" He tweaked his mustache again, a twinkle in his eye.

A young girl was just entering the office with a sheaf of papers for the inspector to sign. She started to giggle, but caught herself. The inspector glanced at her then back at Carlyle and Anna, his face widening into a grin.

Carlyle stepped back into the office and plucked the small cloth bag from the inspector's desk, the bag that had held the snake." Just find out who this belongs to, Inspector, and you will find your murderer."

"Ah, monsieur, but no murder has yet been committed. Unless of course you count the poor snake, who simply died of a 'heart attack', as you say, just as he was ready to strike his victim. Had he succeeded, monsieur, a murder would have been committed and we would have arrested him."

***

"I've taken the liberty of having your trunks picked up and sent on to the villa," Anna said as they drove. "I hope you don't mind? I've had your smaller luggage loaded into the car." She looked over at him, taking her eyes of the road just as they were about to take a winding turn.

"Anna!" Carlyle choked back a scream, just as another car came flying around the bend from the opposite direction. She jerked the wheel just enough to narrowly miss the oncoming car. Carlyle sat gasping for air as she straightened the car and sped off down the narrow stretch of roadway. "Anna, for God's sake, please slow down. And watch the road, will you?"

"Oh, yes darling. Of course, but you've had a frightful day already. What, with the snake and everything."

"And the inspector . . ."

"Yes, such a dreadful little man." She gave Carlyle a sympathetic look, then looked out the windshield, careful to watch the road this time. She reached and switched on the car's lights. The sun had all but completely disappeared in the growing dusk.

  Carlyle sighed, and looked out the window, then leaned his head back on the seat and closed his eyes. The car swerved a little and he opened one eye again, nervously expecting disaster; but things seemed fine. He opened the other eye and looked at Anna. She was still beautiful, just as he had remembered her. Then he closed both of his eyes again, feeling very tired. "So you've spoken to Franz . . ." he said, drifting, wondering just how much Franz would have told her. Would he have told her about the letter, or that Victor was trying to kill Carlyle? Surely not. The whole idea seemed ludicrous. After all, Victor was dead. Franz must have just asked her to meet Carlyle at the train station. Why wouldn't he have met Carlyle himself, though, after sending such an urgent letter? There had to be a logical explanation. The whole situation seemed preposterous, totally absurd. His imagination was just running away with him. First the crazy letter from Franz--That had started him off . . . The snake had been real, of course, but there must be an explanation for

Cobra's Demise

that too. After all, he was still alive. He wasn't quite sure how much longer he could remain that way. The odds certainly didn't seem to be stacked in his favor at the moment.

"Hm? Oh, Franz. Yes, he is at the villa now." She decided that she would have to tell him about Franz soon, prepare him.

"Wake up darling," Anna said. "We've arrived." She shook him again. Finally, Carlyle rubbed his eyes, crawling upward out of the bounds of sleep. "Poor dear, you must be terribly exhausted."

"Mm." Carlyle stretched, pulling himself up out of the car. He had forgotten just how far the villa had been from the nearest town. Perhaps it hadn't been that far. He had been utterly exhausted from traveling.

"I'll get the bags," he said.

"Nonsense. Simon can manage them." She said something in French and a man slipped around them and started to unload the bags. Carlyle hadn't even noticed the man prior to her mentioning him. He wondered for a moment if perhaps the man had been in the car with them the whole time and had just been extremely silent. He decided not. Certainly, he would have noticed him.

Unless, of course, the little man had been packed in his own small bag, popping out just at the proper moment to help carry things.

  Simon was small and wiry and appeared to be about ninety years old, yet he moved with the gracefulness of a cat, or small monkey. His sinewy limbs were nimble and lithe, and he lifted the bags without the slightest hesitation. Carlyle caught sight of the man's face in the rising moonlight; The slant of the dark, inset eyes, and smallish features lent to his mysterious, cat-like appearance. He guessed at Simon's Persian descent, and he also decided he had probably guessed wrong. He then saw that he had misjudged the man's age by about twenty years, though he wasn't sure in which direction. Anna caught Carlyle's sleeve and moved him on toward the villa, seemingly not at all noticing his fixation on the little man. She slid her arm through his as they walked. The large door was held open for them by an extremely large man. The man's bulk blocked the whole doorway. He stepped back out of their way to let them enter. "Good evening, madame, I trust you have had a safe journey."

Cobra's Demise

"Alfred, will you please have Natasha fix our guest something to eat before he retires?" She squeezed Carlyle's arm lovingly when she said "our guest," and warded off any protestations Carlyle might have at the suggestion. As far as Alfred goes, he was definitely British, and had a voice that did not at all fit his large frame. It was as though he were whispering at the very top of his lungs. Carlyle at first thought the man must have had throat surgery at some point, and perhaps he had just misplaced the small mechanical device which helped him speak--The kind one holds against the throat which works on the principle of vibration. Carlyle could not see the small tracheotomy hole though, because there was none. If Alfred was hurt that Anna didn't respond to his inquiry about her journey, he didn't show it. He merely nodded toward Carlyle with a raspy, "Good evening, sir," and then lumbered away to relay instructions to Natasha.

Carlyle looked quickly around for the little man carrying his bags. He had disappeared, or so Carlyle had thought until he spotted the eerie, simian like creature on the staircase at the end of the long hall. The man had just stepped onto the upper landing and then disappeared around the corner. Carlyle caught the man's glance back over his shoulder just before he vanished. It was just a momentary glance from the small dark face. The eyes told Carlyle nothing, just a deadpan look. Perhaps not even a look at all, perhaps Carlyle had only imagined it. He wasn't sure, yet a slight chill slid up his spine.

  Anna led Carlyle quickly into a parlor to the right of the large foyer, and shut the door behind them. No sooner had she flung the door closed than she was in his arms, kissing him passionately. The kiss was relatively short, but had stunned him enough that he was winded when she pulled back. It was something he had longed for since he had first met her several years before. But she had been Victor's girl then, and eventually she had become Victor's wife. He had been forced to hide his true feelings for her due to his lifelong friendship with Victor. These feelings he hadn't even confided to Franz. He and Franz and Victor had been like blood brothers since childhood. He wasn't quite sure how to respond when she eased her lips off of his and

Cobra's Demise

looked at him. She was wide-eyed with anticipation. Her eyes were large, and liquid brown. There was a small light across the room which would have given her eyes a misty sheen had she been turned toward it. Instead, they held the fiery glow from within, a heated passion. "You seem surprised darling," she said. She had him pinned up against the door.

"Well, yes . . . I--I mean, no, I mean, Anna. Really. I . . ."

"Oh, darling. Quit stammering. You're acting like a schoolboy."

He was. He knew that he was but he couldn't help it. He couldn't control himself. "Anna. Victor. What about Victor?"

"Victor?" She stopped, turned away for a moment.

She stepped back from him, trying to control herself.

She gathered herself together and faced him again. "Victor is dead," she said. Then again, more slowly, her voice trembling, "Victor is dead."

Carlyle held out his hand to her. She came into his arms and he held her, comforting her. They stood together for several minutes, holding each other.

Carlyle thought about the last time he had seen her, of that morning at breakfast. He buried his nose in her hair. The scent of her consumed him, the same scent of that morning. He thought of that morning as if it were a dream, her leaning over him to push the curtains further open, Victor waking them by hollering about the window, and her whispering something in his ear. He thought about Victor. Yes, of course. Victor *was* dead. Victor was his friend, but Victor was dead. All this nonsense about Victor trying to kill him was surely just that, just nonsense. Why would Victor want him dead? They had been friends-- more than friends—brothers; or as close as any three brothers could be. . . he, Victor, and Franz. And he had always been fond of Anna, and she had been just as fond of him. It was something they had both always known, but had never mentioned. Their feelings had always remained unspoken. Now there was no reason to hide it, he realized. Nor was there any reason to feel guilty. Victor was dead. Anna raised her face to his.

Cobra's Demise

They kissed. The door suddenly pushed open behind them, the handle jamming into Carlyle's kidney. There was a loud crash. The serving girl, Natasha, had dropped Carlyle's dinner onto the floor. Anna flew into a rage. It was a side of her that Carlyle had never seen. Natasha seemed to tremble in Anna's presence. She was thin, almost to the point of being anorexic, and very pallid. Her eyes were large and would normally have been very beautiful had it not been for the large shadows around them. She appeared very nervous, and tense. Carlyle would have guessed that she hadn't slept in days.

Natasha was Russian, and her French was only passable. Her English was a little better, though she spoke with a stutter. The stutter was probably just from her being so nervous. Carlyle's heart went out to her in her plight. Anna seemed exceptionally cruel to her, calling her a stupid Russian. She immediately ordered the girl to fix a new tray. Carlyle protested, saying that he really hadn't been all that hungry anyway; but Anna refused to listen. Simon appeared on the scene with a mop and bucket, literally popping out of nowhere.

Carlyle lie in bed later, still thinking about the dinner situation. Perhaps he dwelled upon this as it seemed to be the only normal event of his day. Everything else seemed far too bizarre, what with the snake and the inspector and all. It seemed rather commonplace in light of the rest. Anna's sudden change of behavior had surprised him though. He honestly felt that she had been far too rough on Natasha for having dropped his dinner. After all, the girl couldn't have known that they were all but leaning against the door when she tried to open it. She was simply doing what she had been instructed to do. Perhaps she should have knocked first, before entering, but that had been her only fault. Anna had been quite rough on her in Carlyle's view. The girl had obviously been sorry, and she had apologized to no end. He made up his mind to mention this to Anna the next day. He vowed to say something on the girl's behalf anyway.

One thing that struck Carlyle as particularly odd was that the whole household seemed to be a smorgasbord of international misfits. And that man Simon positively gave him the creeps. He made up his mind to avoid the man as much as possible during his stay.

Cobra's Demise

Carlyle thought of all that had transpired since his last visit. Nothing seemed to make the least bit of sense. It was the urgent letter from Franz that had brought him to the villa in such a rush. The letter had been ambiguous in all but one respect: It made a point of being perfectly clear about Victor's intention to kill Carlyle. Which didn't make any sense at all since Victor had passed on two months prior. Even if the preposterous idea were true, why meet at the villa? That would be the most likely place to meet up with Victor if he were still alive. It didn't add up.

All else in the letter had seemed mere ramblings of a mad man. The handwriting had been Franz's, yet very much unlike Franz in content. And where was Franz? Anna had been somewhat vague when he had questioned her as to Franz's whereabouts. She had merely brushed him off with the answer that yes, Franz was at the villa, but that he had taken ill and was lying down. She would not comment further, except to assure Carlyle that he could speak with Franz on the morrow.

What if Victor were still alive? Carlyle suddenly thought. The idea jolted him. That would be fantastic, his friend still alive. Other than the notion that he would be trying to kill him, it cheered Carlyle.

He lay in bed pondering all of these strange ideas, all the day's odd events, including the bizarre incident with the snake, and touching on each of the characters he had met that evening in the household, and he became restless. He was beginning to think that his imagination was getting the best of him. Or perhaps part of his not being able to fall asleep was simply due to his nap in the car. In either case, he tossed and turned for a seemingly endless period of time.

After much tossing about, he finally switched on the bedside lamp and sat up. A mouse scampered into a far corner of the room and disappeared from sight. Carlyle looked at his watch on the bedside table: ten past one. He pulled out the letter again.

Carlyle had just begun to read the letter over when he thought he heard voices in the hall. He wouldn't have given them much consideration had it not been so late, and had not one of the voices been rising in pitch and protestation. He extinguished the bedside lamp then went to the bedroom door, opening it a crack. He could barely make out one shadow in the darkened hallway, but it appeared to be Natasha. He could not make out the voice nor countenance of the other party. Natasha was protesting something in a sibilant but rising and fearful tone. "I cannot," she was saying. "Please, no. Please. I cannot do it." There was a word muttered from the one to whom she was speaking, a final tonality. From the resigned sigh of her body, she appeared to give in and there was no more. She stood momentarily in the hallway, crossing herself and muttering something in Russian, and then she turned and went to what Carlyle surmised to be her room at the end of the hall. The other party had disappeared immediately after uttering the final authoritative word to the girl. Well, "disappeared" might be a bit of an exaggeration considering Carlyle could not see the other party to begin with. In any case, the hall became silent again. Carlyle closed his door and went back to his bed, feeling somewhat guilty at having eavesdropped. He immediately forgot his guilt when he stubbed his toe against the bedpost in the darkness. "Ow, Oh, Jeez--" He bit his lip to keep from crying out. Just what you bloody well deserve, he thought, for spying on people in the middle of the night. After dancing round for a time, he fell back on the bed, forgetting the letter until he felt crunching paper beneath him. He pulled it out from under him and tossed it toward the bedstand, losing all desire to read it. And as the throbbing subsided in his toe, he gradually fell asleep.

It was two and a half hours later when Carlyle was awakened from a fitful sleep. He had been dreaming a horrid dream he was sure; though he couldn't quite remember what it was. There was a moaning, he remembered quite clearly, and such a pathetic whimpering, rising to an almost unbearable pitch. One could not quite be certain whether the sound was man or beast. It sounded again, a wretched, shrill-like scream that droned on into the night, almost inhuman. And the clawing, and thudding, as though someone or something were hurling itself against the wall. He suddenly realized that the sounds were real and coming from the next room. His heart lurched and pounded at the sound. Certainly, the walls were not that thin? The railings and carryings-on were increasing in intensity. He jumped from the bed and ran to his door, flinging it wide and starting into the hall. Suddenly fearful, he looked around for something with which to defend

Cobra's Demise

himself, but found nothing. The sounds came again, a pleading, begging moan, then almost a sob. Carlyle approached the room from which the sounds emerged. It was the room adjacent to his own as he had suspected. There was a key in the lock on the hall side of the door, and the door stood slightly ajar. Carlyle pushed it open, cautiously, fearful of attack from whatever lie within. He was in no way prepared for what he saw, nor the stench of human odor which struck him squarely in the face: perspiration, urine, vomit and feces. A being very much like Franz, yet very unlike Franz, stared up at him, but only for a second. The rest was a blur, all happening very quickly. Natasha turned to face him, caught off guard, a look of stunned fear in her eyes. Yet the fear in her eyes could not even begin to match the terror in the Franz creature's eyes, nor the horror running through Carlyle's own mind. He caught the movement of drapery billowing inward momentarily, just in the corner of his eye, then the Franz-like blur racing toward it and proceeding straight on through. In a moment so surreal, yet so terrible, he could not even begin to have imagined it, he moved instinctively after the figure that had once been his friend. He was right on the being's heels, grasping, clawing, a flailing of arms. Franz tripped and fell, Carlyle falling over him. Then he was up again, a flurry of arms and legs. Carlyle reaching, grasping a pant leg, ripping the cuff. The fingernails of his other hand ran the length of Franz's arm, fingers touching fingers, but grasping nothing as Franz plunged on over the rail's ledge, falling three stories to his death.

Carlyle coughed and choked, gasped for air, started to his knees, then fell back, unbelieving. He looked around. The girl was gone. In her place stood Anna, and just behind Anna, the simian form of Simon. The only two missing were the girl and the butler. Another woman appeared, a sturdy woman, with a menacing look about her. Carlyle had not seen this woman before. He didn't bother with trying to figure out who she was. He guessed there were perhaps others he had not seen yet, who might also be in Anna's employ. It did seem quite singular, and he wasn't quite sure why it hit him at that particular moment, that the whole time prior to Victor's death there had only been but one housekeeper at the villa that he had been aware of, a German woman by the name of Frau Furstburg; and she was no longer around. Yet what did it matter, for here were many others to take her place.

***

"WHAT? Surely you cannot be serious! Murder?! You are accusing me of Murder?"

"Accusing is a strong word, monsieur. Certainly, you can understand the--"

"Murder is a strong word. A nasty word, a bugger of a word. Surely you can't be serious. I am not a murderer. Franz was my friend. I was merely trying to--"

"To save him, yes I know. But you see monsieur, until we find the girl, well?" With that the inspector shrugged his shoulders.

"That's it? That's bloody it? You're going to lock me up like a common criminal? The girl's probably halfway back to Siberia by now. She's the one you need to be after."

"Perhaps," was the inspector's only reply as he stood patiently watching Carlyle rant and rave behind the bars of the small cell.

"Perhaps? That's all you have to say? Perhaps?"

The inspector looked blank. "Perhaps," he shrugged "Perhaps not."

Carlyle stood gaping at the inspector, disbelieving. The diminutive inspector watched him. How could the man be so idiotic? thought Carlyle. He paced away from the cell bars, glancing at another man sleeping on a bench along the side wall of the small cell, a drunk, the only other man in the cell. The man snored loudly and stunk badly. Carlyle seemed to just now notice him. Carlyle glanced back at the cell bars, expecting the inspector to be gone. He felt like a caged animal. The inspector was still there, watching him. He started to open his mouth again, pleading his case. The inspector interrupted him before he even got started. "You cannot deny, monsieur, that those around you have died under very suspicious circumstances, no?"

Carlyle wasn't sure who the inspector meant by the word "those." The impression seemed to be that there had been many, as though Carlyle had brought back from India with him some mysterious plague, and that people were dying off left and right wherever he went. "Oh, come now, Inspector, the snake?"

"Precisely my point, monsieur, neither man nor beast is safe in your presence. Perhaps I should move Jacques to another cell? See how he trembles, in fear for his life? Carlyle did not even glance over to where the other man lay snoring. He merely glared at the inspector. The inspector just shrugged his shoulders and smirked before turning away.

"Just ring up Colin Wexford, in London, Inspector. We'll see who has the last laugh." He walked away from the bars, looking for a place to sit. He suddenly was very tired, yet still quite angry. "Bloody little twit," he muttered, kicking out at the other bench in the cell. He had completely forgotten his sore toe and almost screamed out in pain when it connected with the bench. It brought tears to his eyes.

It wasn't long before Carlyle lay in a daze, begrudgingly accepting his fate. His anger had subsided. The sweat and stink of the cell had become monotonous. Eventually, even the dirty drunk's snoring had somehow lulled him. At first it had been annoying. He had lain there staring at the fat man's dirty belly which rose and fell with each intake and outlet of air under the dirty, sweat-soaked t-shirt. Then he had rolled over on the uncomfortable bench and stared at the wall. There was a long crack in the wall. He followed it to where it split off, one branch reaching down toward the floor, the other branch going a ways off to the right and then petering out. Someone had carved the word "MERDE" into the wall, a short distance above the top branch of the crack. My sentiments exactly, he thought. There was an obscene rhyme carved closer to the floor. The privy was a hulk of hollowed out metal in the far corner. He dreaded the thought of having to use it. Hopefully not, he thought. He prayed that somehow the silly little inspector would come to his senses and subsequently release him. Soon he had fallen steadfastly asleep, his own rhythmic breathing coinciding with the rise and fall of Jacque's large, dirty belly.

Eventually, after several more hours, Carlyle woke to the sound of the cell doors swinging open. He wasn't at first aware of what was happening, or where he was. He heard the keys rattle, rubbed his eyes and looked up in the now dim cell to see the custodian of the cell poking Jacques in the ribs, trying to wake him. Jacques tried to push the stick away, angry that his slumber was being disturbed. The man poked him again, telling Jacques that his wife had come to take him home. Jacques sat up, slowly, after fighting off the stick a few more times. Finally, the custodian got him to his feet. He stood up groaning, letting forth a stream of obscenities directed mainly at his wife for being the cause of his sleep being disturbed. He scratched his head and belched. He looked absently at Carlyle, then at the door to the cell. He scratched his large belly, moving awkwardly toward the cell door. He exited, leaving the solitude of the cell behind him. The doors swung closed again, and the silence became deafening, bringing Carlyle fully up out of the bounds of sleep. He lay awake then, waiting in the darkness. Waiting for what? He wondered.

Carlyle could do nothing now save ponder the predicament he now found himself in. He all at once realized how totally ignorant he was of French law, especially with regard to murder. He suddenly felt completely helpless, and he missed his cellmate, truly, without condescension. How simple Jacques' life was compared to what his own had become. How simple his own life had been prior to receiving the letter from Franz. He started there and wound through the thoughts, actions and circumstances, which lead up to this very moment. Poor Franz, having died so, and in such a wretched state just prior to his death. How had he come to that? And it was all so absurd that Carlyle himself could be thought the murderer. He let his mind wander over lingering possibilities. Suppose Victor was still alive and behind it all somehow? Nonsense. Carlyle wouldn't believe it. Certainly, when they found the Russian girl the truth would out. If they found the girl. A sense of panic rose up from the pit of his stomach. He tried to calm himself. He started again through the whole of all the events, taking them one at a time, this time going all the way back to the last time he had seen Victor. . .

  Victor had been a much different man the last few months before his death, or at least the last time Carlyle had seen him, radically different. Along with his angry outbursts, there would be alternate periods, interludes of calm. One such instance occurred after dinner on the evening just prior to Carlyle's departure. Carlyle had heard Victor playing his violin, and he had followed the music into the study. He sat across from Victor and listened with great interest to Victor's playing. After a while, Victor stopped. Carlyle complimented him on the fact that he had not lost his touch, not with music, nor women. To this last remark he added that Anna was still exceptionally beautiful, and that she appeared to be as much in love as ever. Victor looked mildly

Cobra's Demise

puzzled at first, but it passed, and Carlyle let it. Whatever *it* was, neither men pursued. They went on to other talk, small talk of past events. Franz soon joined them, and they had great fun rehashing old stories. It was apparently one of Victor's more lucid moments and he seemed to be enjoying the company, but then a change came over him. Toward the end of the evening he began withdrawing into himself again, becoming more and more despondent. Finally, they each exchanged goodnights and went to bed. Carlyle knew he would not be returning to see Victor on any future trips, if nothing more than by choice. He couldn't bear to see his friend losing out to the battle with cancer. Victor was the strong one of their group. He had done a fine job of fighting the disease. He had put up a very good battle and had even gone into remission a time or two over the past three years; but the resignation showed. The battle was lost.

Carlyle had felt a little guilty of his decision not to return, but was sure he wouldn't blame either of the others if the situation were reversed. It was the next morning that Victor had thrown his fit about the window. All in all, it had been a very minor incident; yet Carlyle kept coming back to it time and again.

Perhaps it was simply because it was the last time that he had seen Victor alive. He was sure that was all it was and that there was nothing more to it.

In any event, Carlyle left the villa and hadn't returned until he received the letter from Franz. He should have tried harder to return for the funeral perhaps, but that couldn't be helped now.

As far as more current events went, the letter from Franz was missing when he got back to his room, after the scuffle with Franz. It had conveniently vanished. Convenient for whom? The murderer, he supposed. That made sense. In any case it had mysteriously disappeared, right along with the Russian girl, at the time of Franz's death. His thoughts, again and again came back to the girl, no matter where he started in his thinking. That was the snag, the dead end. Always her face, always the fear that she would not be found. Of course, they would find her. And if not? Well, if not . . .? It would do him no good to worry, he told himself, and then he proceeded right on doing it. Certainly, Colin Wexford would be coming to his rescue. And there was Anna, of course. She would be trying everything in her power to procure his release. She would be by to see him in the morning he was quite sure. She had told him she was sorry and . . . Carlyle felt something tug at the corner of his mind. He couldn't grasp it at the moment. Reluctantly curious as to what it might be, but at a loss as to how to ferret it out, he let it go, hoping it would come back around like an errant child on a merry-go-round.

At any rate, Anna would, of course, have her own lawyers and . . . Something scurried quickly through the darkness, moving from the cell floor, across the top of Carlyle's foot. He sat bolt upright, several horrifyingly distinct thoughts being triggered at once by the rodent, as though a mechanism had been released in his brain, suddenly making everything perfectly clear. Carlyle jumped from the bench and almost fell in the floor due to his sleeping leg. He dragged it behind him, pounding it with his fist, trying to stop the tingling sensation, or else at least hurry it along. He lunged for the cell bars. "Inspector!" he yelled at the top of his lungs. "Inspector . . . Ring up the Inspector!"

***

"Well?" said the inspector. "Now that you have interrupted my dinner; What is so important that it could not wait until the morning? You have taken on the job of inspector and solved the case, no?" He stood outside the cell door, the dim light from the outer office touching lightly upon his neck and the side of his face. He was wearing a dinner jacket, and his hair was slicked back, looking very neat and dapper. He smoothed a hand down over his mustache, and then sighed, waiting.

"Well, yes. I mean, no. I haven't taken over as inspector, but—I've figured it out. I know who the murderer is . . .

"That is something we have determined also monsieur, well before your arrival."

Carlyle was a bit confused, perhaps even stunned by the inspector's statement.

"So let us hear your theory, monsieur, and then perhaps you can help us with a little problem . . ."

***

"I'm so happy that that nasty little inspector released you, darling," Anna said as she walked toward Carlyle with the two glasses of wine. "What a dreadful little man." The two of them stood in the parlor where they had been when the Russian girl had bumped into them. They were almost in the very spot. Anna handed Carlyle one glass of the wine and kept one for herself. "How could he have possibly thought you pushed Franz to his death? It

Cobra's Demise

was, of course, that little wretch of a Russian girl. It was entirely her fault. How could Franz have gotten involved with her to begin with? I don't even know why I hired her. She's been nothing but trouble. Carlyle set his wine almost immediately down upon the top of the piano which was the closest flat surface within reach. He was wary of Anna now, knew her tricks. She came closer. "Poor dear Franz," she said, true pity resonating in her voice. "Poor, poor, Franz. And Victor." She paused. Almost too casually, she suggested Carlyle take a drink of wine. She put her own glass to her lips.

"I'll just drink yours," Carlyle said suddenly. It wasn't very subtle, but it was effective.

A flicker of acknowledgment passed over Anna's face. Her eyes danced nervously, but only for a second. She obviously knew Carlyle was on to her, yet she continued to play the game. She shrugged and handed him the glass. A tear rolled down her cheek. "I am sorry for Victor, and also for Franz. You are the only one left, love." He had gone from darling to love very quickly. "You and I, we're the only ones left. We need each other.

"Cut the act, Anna," Carlyle said. He was sure that the inspector had had enough time by now to have retrieved the Russian girl. Looking Anna straight in the eyes, he bravely downed her glass of wine. He was quite certain she wouldn't have put a tainted glass to her own lips. "Is this how you got Franz hooked on the morphine? Did you taint his wine with a sleeping powder and then shoot him up with the stuff? Or did you simply get him drunk and wait until he passed out.

"But darling," she said. "I love you. Don't you see? Don't you understand? We can be together now." She touched her fingers to his cheek, casually moving them up and down caressingly.

Carlyle ignored her fingers and continued: "Or did you just seduce him, and then shoot him up after making passionate love to him, once his eyes blissfully closed? Tell me, Anna, how did you do it?" Her fingers then traveled up and through his hair. Her liquid brown eyes were softly melting. She had her arms round Carlyle's neck, kissing him. He began to want her; he had always wanted her. He stopped himself, shaking his head. He pulled her arms from round his neck. "I know about you Anna, about your plans, your murders." He looked at her, her eyes, expecting her to give in and show some sign of surprise or shock at his knowing all about her. She showed nothing, gave him nothing to go on. He was afraid for a moment that he was seriously on the wrong track, that he had been dreadfully wrong about her. Maybe she hadn't killed Victor after all? Maybe she hadn't gotten Franz strung out on morphine? Maybe she hadn't planned on killing them both because Victor had left the estate to all three of them instead of just to her?

Carlyle felt quite confused all of a sudden. He continued on the planned tack though, for lack of a better plan. "You forgot, Anna, we all have the same solicitor, Colin Wexford; or had you intended to kill him also? Of course, he had already contacted Franz, and Franz came to tell you that no matter what Victor had wanted, he was willing to give up his share to you. But you didn't give him the chance to tell you, did you Anna? And I would have given up my share also, Anna, willingly. I have my own trust, as had Franz his. Of course, Franz's trust wasn't as generous as mine. I don't know if I could have been quite so magnanimous as Franz, had I been in his shoes. But that was just the kind of person that Franz was. You were simply blinded by greed, Anna. No one can really blame you for that. You had come up on the wrong side of the tracks, and you didn't want to go back. Being a simple hired nurse wasn't good enough. Victor had taken you to heart when he became ill with cancer. He had taken you into his home and given freely to you. He loved you. He married you. But that wasn't good enough was it? He wasn't dying quick enough for you was he? You took it upon yourself to hasten his death with lethal doses of morphine . . . morphine . . . just as you planned with Franz. But I helped you along with Franz, didn't I? Lucky for you. I don't know what he was so afraid of? Or had you so gotten his mind twisted on drugs that he didn't know what he was doing, even when he wrote me the letter? Did you have him believing I was Victor, back from the dead, coming to kill him, and myself? I . . . I" Carlyle's mind seemed to be going numb on him. "You made a mistake, Anna, when you jokingly suggested giving Victor an extra dose of medicine to end his tirade. Remember Anna, at breakfast that morning, the morning of my last visit? Remember whispering it to me as you leaned across to open the curtains? Was that when you first thought of it? Hm? Please God, Anna, tell me it was a mercy killing. Tell me you just couldn't stand to see the poor dear bastard suffer. Please tell me it wasn't just for plain old

Cobra's Demise

greed." Anna looked away, self-consciously, not holding his eye. A momentary pang of guilt perhaps. "It wasn't, was it, Anna? Please tell me it wasn't. Not just for greed, please. And later . . . later . . ." Carlyle was feeling really drowsy. He gave a big yawn. His eyes kept closing. "The. . . snake . . . the snake, was he supposed to scare me . . . off . . . or, or kill . . . me?" Carlyle's eyes closed again. He could not keep them open. He had to keep fluttering his eyelids, as though he were exercising them. He couldn't keep them open long enough now to see exactly what Anna was doing. She had moved across the room and Carlyle heard a drawer open. She came back over to him. He was still flitting his eyes, working his jaw, anything to try and remain awake. He could just make out split second images as the opening and closing of his eye moved like the aperture of a camera, only more slowly, much more slowly.

He heard Anna laugh as she pulled the cap off of the syringe. She paused, looking at him. "The snake," she said. "He was supposed to kill you. I merely misjudged the poor creature's metabolism." She filled the syringe and thumped it. Testing it, she shot a few drops into the air.

"The . . . wine . . ." Carlyle slid down the door, and onto the floor.

"Yes darling, the wine. I was on to you first thing."

Carlyle muttered something more.

"Hm, what's that darling?"

"The kil . . . killing . . . when . . . end?" Carlyle was trying to reach up and knock the needle out of her hand as he spoke. His arm was like lead. He couldn't lift it. Anna had the needle poised above him.

"Very soon, darling. It will all end very soon." She was next to him on the floor, turning his arm round for the injection. Of course, just jabbing him in the neck would have gotten the job done, but some of the delicacies of being a trained nurse died hard. The door burst open suddenly, slamming into her arm and sending the needle flying across the floor. She pounced upon it and was up in a flash, charging the Inspector. He was having a hard time getting completely into the room due to Carlyle's body lying in the path of the door. But when Anna charged, the diminutive man moved with split second timing and deflected her joust quickly enough to send the needle plunging into the door frame where it broke. So much for the nursing delicacies.

Cobra's Demise

"Madame, you are under arrest for murder," the Inspector blurted out excitedly, his voice rising too high in pitch. He cleared his throat and repeated himself. Apparently, he just then realized how close he had come to being stabbed with a needle full of morphine. Anna was momentarily stunned with the surprise of her miss; and had just started to attack the man again when a large, well-tailored arm shot through the doorway and grabbed her. It was Alfred. "Take her away," said the Inspector. Anna was protesting heavily as Alfred dragged her through the half open door.

The inspector leaned down and checked Carlyle's pulse. He raised one of Carlyle's eyelids, then the other. "Hm," he said. "Sleeping." He stood up, spotting the glass of wine on the piano. "I warned you about the wine, monsieur. I told you to suspect anything she offered." He picked up the glass and held it up to the light. He sniffed it, and rolled the wine round in the glass. He spied the half full bottle and went over to it, "Mon dieu," he exclaimed, reading the label. "A vintage to be savoured." He looked down at Carlyle, spotting the empty glass on the floor. It had broken in the fall, but wasn't completely shattered. "You merely chose the wrong one, mon ami." With that, he took a sip from the full glass, swishing the wine over his tongue and around his mouth, pausing to experience the taste more completely. He then swallowed, positively glowing with the effect. "Tres bon." He finished off the rest of the wine from the glass and then grabbed the bottle and headed out the door, muttering something about evidence and delicately stepping over Carlyle as he went.

***

"I understand you had quite a rest, hm, Inspector?" Carlyle prodded him two days later. "Apparently Anna laced both the glasses with sleeping powder as an extra precaution. I was a bit too quick in stopping her and switching glasses. She had put the glass to her lips, but she didn't have time to drink. With either one she would have had me. As it was, she had us both." Carlyle grinned. The inspector merely looked at Carlyle, failing to see the humor. After a moment of gloating, Carlyle continued: "So the funny looking little man, Simon, also works for you?"

"Oui, monsieur, along with the Russian girl, Natasha, and also Alfred, my best man. We have had Madame Bonaducce under surveillance for quite

Cobra's Demise

some time. We suspected that she had murdered her husband, but we had no proof. We were keeping a very close watch."

"The night of Franz's death, Inspector, what happened there? Who was the girl, Natasha, speaking with, in the hall?"

"Alfred. It seems that she was afraid the shot she was to give your friend, Franz, was an overdose. She had been worried for several days. The man was very much hooked on the morphine. He needed medical attention. We were going to remove him the next day from the villa. We were working on a plan. In the meantime, the girl needed to play along and give your friend a shot periodically, to keep him from falling apart or dying before we got him out. The woman, Anna, had completely changed his thinking with the drug after only a short time. The girl was fearful of giving him the shot that night. She was afraid that the woman had administered far too much. And she was correct. So, you see, your friend was to die that night no matter what happened. Had you not interrupted the process of Natasha giving him the shot, he would have died anyway. Had the girl not given him the shot he would probably . . . well, who is to say what would or would not have happened. But you understand my meaning, no? Natasha's mistake had been in unlocking and opening the window before giving him the shot. He grabbed the works from her and ran. Had the girl not given him the shot, as she did not, it would not have mattered either way. She would have been found out in her hesitation. The girl could not win.

The woman had suspected her. It was a setup, monsieur. Had the girl administered the shot to your friend, she would have technically become the murderer, and you would have been the witness." The inspector paused, looking at Carlyle. "So you see," he continued, "you saved the girl."

"And then lost her," Carlyle said.

"Oui, monsieur, a temporary inconvenience. You helped us find her again before it was too late. Apparently, the woman had still hoped to use her as the murder suspect, in case you were cleared. And of course, monsieur, I did not really think you had killed anyone, but was merely holding you, for your own safety of course, until we found the girl." He paused again. "But tell me, how did you know of the secret room?"

"Oh, Franz, Victor, and I stumbled upon it a years ago, as teens. I had completely forgotten about it until I remembered how easily the sound had traveled to me from Franz's room. The story was that there had been an old Jewish man who lived in the villa during the war. He was understandably afraid for his life with the Nazis marching into Paris. He had the wall reconstructed. Apparently, he put up a new, fake wall, making its width triple the normal size width. He couldn't make it too wide, and chance spoiling the illusion of it being anything more than just a wall. He finished it off by putting in the secret door from the hall, and the passageway between the walls. Of course, you saw how narrow the passage was, you had to turn sideways to get down the stairs. Fine as children, but . . . Anyway, there was no other way into the secret room in the cellar which the old man took pains to build, and equip with essential supplies. You went down the three flights of very narrow stairs and voila. But, alas, the Germans bypassed the villa altogether.

"And Anna must have found it later; or perhaps Victor had told her about it. It was very hard to just stumble onto it. We did as children, of course, but children tend to be more curious than adults . . . so that really was where the Russian girl had gotten off to? So, as I was scuffling with Franz, Anna's accomplice was busy secreting the girl in the hidden room. She must have chloroformed her to keep her from screaming out. She was not an exceptionally small woman from what I saw. I suspect she had quite the time on those narrow stairs, especially maneuvering the girl down, in front or from behind, whichever may have been the case, neither must have been easy. And this was the same woman who showed up on the scene shortly thereafter, with Anna. She made very quick work of the girl, I must say. Who is she?"

"We don't know exactly; just someone Madame Bonaducce had recruited on her own. I will question her more this afternoon."

"You mean a legitimate housekeeper in Anna's employ?"

The inspector merely smiled at this. "Oui, and it seems we have now recovered the body of the original housekeeper. She was the woman who first sounded the alarm, and pointed the finger at Madame Bonaducce, before mysteriously vanishing.

"Is there simply no end to murder?"

"There is now, it seems, mon ami, at least in this case. The two men looked at each other in silence for a moment, as though congratulating one another on a job well done and wondering what to do next. The inspector touched a finger to his temple and then pulled a telegram from his desk drawer, handing it to Carlyle. The telegram was from Colin Wexford. Carlyle read it over carefully. It informed him that he was now the sole heir of Victor's entire estate, the villa included. It made him a little uneasy. "What about Anna?" he asked.

"I am afraid, madame will not have any use for the villa now."

"Pity."

The inspector raised one eyebrow in surprise and tweaked his mustache. "May I remind you, mon ami, that the woman tried to murder you, twice."

"I'm quite aware of that, Inspector," said Carlyle. He seemed a little pained at having been reminded. Rather than try and explain the fact that Anna had once upon a time been a very warm and generous woman, had at one time in fact had a heart, and was not then quite as greedy as she had somehow become, he let it pass. He guessed he truly had been in love with her, at least to some degree, and probably more than he cared to admit now.

"Ah, yes," the inspector sighed. "Women." With that he started shuffling papers on his desk, and Carlyle rose to leave. When Carlyle was almost to the door, the inspector stopped him. "Tell me again about the snake monsieur."

Carlyle shrugged. "A simple feeding process really. I have seen it done many times in my travels through India, the snake charmers feeding their pets—sans morphine, of course. I had probably even written about it to Victor at one time or another. He was always fascinated with such things. How Anna got hold of a cobra is anyone's guess. Anyway, she injected a mouse with the morphine and fed it to the Cobra. It would have taken several hours for the snake to fully digest the morphine infected rodent. He would have swallowed it whole and then digested it bit by bit. She waited a predetermined number of hours and found a way to slip the snake-in-bag into my railway compartment with the opening loosened just enough. The snake, had Anna timed it right, would have bitten me and then died of a morphine overdose about the same time I expired from his venomous bite; or shortly thereafter, as soon as it had digested enough of the mouse. At this point she could have retrieved the snake easily from the compartment and mine would have been a very curious death indeed. Or, she could have left the snake, since it was then rendered harmless, no matter. It was sheer luck that she had misjudged the metabolism of the snake and it died before striking. Though it was much too close a call. It could have easily turned out to be the perfect plan."

"Ingenious!" The inspector cried out, his eyes all but gleaming.

"Yes, almost."

"You truly are le snake docteur, monsieur," the inspector grinned, totally overwhelmed with admiration.

Carlyle shook his head. "Au revoir, inspector." He then headed out of the inspector's office and on past the girl at the front desk, stopping at the door to give her a wink. She smiled, and he stepped out into the warm afternoon sun, feeling lighter of step than he had felt in days. He heaved a big sigh of relief that the situation was now over, and thought perhaps he might make other arrangements home than by rail.

A week or so later, Carlyle received word from the inspector which shed even more light on things: Anna's mysterious housekeeper turned out to be an

American woman named Wilma Reese. INTERPOL had a red notice out on her. She was wanted in at least five different countries on drug smuggling charges. She had previously travelled round the world with the circus, where she had been billed as "The woman of one thousand and one snakes." She would wrap the snakes round her body, completely covering herself with them as though the reptiles were a suit of clothes, fascinating audiences far and wide.

Well, that explained Anna's newly found snake handling capabilities, and probably also how she acquired the cobra. The woman could have been Anna's morphine supplier also, though Carlyle suspected Anna had merely had drugs left from Victor's last days. The fact that she was a nurse should have told him straight off that she was the one who had supplied Franz with the drug. He had suspected, but did not want to believe it. It was far too easy to believe the Russian girl was at fault, considering he had caught her preparing to give Franz the injection. One can't always believe what one sees.

Carlyle hadn't suspected Victor as having died from anything but cancer, even though Anna had

Cobra's Demise

jokingly spoken of her plans that morning at breakfast. He still felt that she hadn't actually planned it then. Perhaps the idea had only just popped into her head at that point; and she planned it later, after more serious consideration. His feelings for her must have blocked this out of his mind. Strange. Everything seemed to be pointing directly at her, and as the inspector had said, they had previously been well aware of who the murderer had been.

As far as his incident with the snake went, there was no way Carlyle could have connected that with her initially. Although it would explain her being at the train station, and then her locating him at the inspector's office. He had just assumed Franz had sent her to pick him up. Well, the letter would have helped her. As Carlyle had finally suspected later; and she made no attempt to deny having coerced Franz into the writing of it. The letter had merely been a desperate ruse to get Carlyle to the villa, and within reach. She obviously wanted to get to him before Colin Wexford informed him of his entitlement to one third of Victor's estate. Wexford had been unable to contact him previously as he had been away in India. Anna must have decided it too dangerous to have Carlyle die of a morphine overdose at the villa, for that was also how she planned to do in Franz. And of course, Victor had died there also, though his death could have been disguised as natural, the cancer.

But the villa would have still been out of the question as the place for Carlyle to be murdered. Anna and Wilma must have then cooked up the plan with the snake on the train. But what if it hadn't worked? Which obviously it hadn't, thank God. But what if Carlyle had been facing the compartment door when Anna had opened it? And it had been Anna, though he hadn't figured it out until the evening in the jail cell. Would she have come in the compartment and sat talking casually to him with the snake loosened in the bag? He guessed not. It wouldn't have mattered if he had seen her, had the plan worked, he decided. She could have dropped the cobra in the compartment and run, closing the door behind her. In such close quarters, there would have been slim chance of his getting past the snake in order to get to the door.

Yes, that night in the cell probably had saved his life. Amazing how the mind works, thoughts and images shifting, hiding and then coming to light.

Cobra's Demise

There was something in the way Anna always pronounced the word "Sorry." He had never really noticed it before. It's not that the word came across as insincere when it passed her lips; but she definitely had a very distinct and peculiar way of saying it. She always seemed to hesitate right in the middle of its pronunciation. While there is a definite change in syllable right in the center of the word, most people glide through it unnoticeably as "Sa-Ree." Anna, on the other hand, always seemed to hesitate in between the syllables. Her pronunciation was always more of a "Sa-h-Ree." Although she managed to deepen her voice, or disguise it somewhat; when she opened the compartment door on the train, she did not, or perhaps could not, change the way she pronounced the word.

THE EARLY ONES

It was early when he heard the nurse come in, too early. His mouth was dry. He hadn't opened his eyes yet. It seemed almost impossible to do so. Somehow the nurse, or whatever they called them these days, Care givers? He didn't know, didn't care. So he wasn't a caregiver, he guessed. No need to be bitter, he thought.

"Well, there you are," the nurse said. He was going to call her that anyway. It was easier. Where was he supposed to have been? He was quite sure he hadn't been anywhere else. He couldn't leave the damn bed. Never would again. But he knew what she meant. How did she know he was awake? He had been on the edges of sleep, or the drug-induced state they kept him in. He must have moved slightly, or groaned. "Rise and shine," she continued. Enough, he thought. Enough. He wanted to tell her to go to hell. He knew he wasn't going to get up and leave the bed. She knew it. He knew she knew it. And he suspected she knew that he knew she knew it. He wanted to chuckle at that train of thought. He didn't. Every hospice patient felt like this, he supposed. Probably even the ones that were totally out of it. He wasn't quite out of it completely, not yet. "Early bird gets the worm."

Early bird gets the worm? They had this woman in the wrong place. You wanted the caregiver, or nurse to be upbeat, yes, but this was ridiculous. All the same, the phrase took him back. Back to when his mother and father used to try and wake him up in the mornings. Didn't matter whether it was so he could go to school, or go find a Christmas tree. He left the nurse do her thing; rummaging around, fumbling with things. He was back in childhood

The Early Ones

now. He, his father and two sisters were trudging through the snow, searching out the best tree. It was late 50's or early in the 60's. Couldn't be any later than 1966, because that was the year they had moved south, far south. There would be some snow then, some years. Not often and not much, only an inch or two, and it would be gone in a day or so. No, this had to be when they still lived up in the Midwest. A lot of snow. It was always fun then. Going to get the tree. He wasn't sure how exciting it had been for his father, but he guessed maybe some excitement was there. They always had to have a live tree. Even after moving south. Of course, trees were more abundant there anyway. So it was easier. So there they would be, or were, trudging through the snow, looking for the perfect tree. He believed this memory was from the same year they got the toboggan for Christmas. So he was about five years old then. Man, tobogganing, the *swoosh* of flying down the slope. The cold biting your face, nose running. Or he guessed the proper way to say it was "Jack Frost nipping at your nose." So where did it all go, the time. And then he had a thought, Nowhere! Time would still be. He would be gone, but it would still be. He was awake now, and in some pain. The morphine must be wearing off. The nurse shifted the pillow beneath him to make him comfortable. More pain. "Comfortable?" she asked. Hell no. She just made it worse. He grimaced and held his breath for a second. He would love to slap her, but that would only make the pain worse for him, even if he could raise his arm to do it. She had leaned in close to adjust his pillow. He got a strong whiff of her perfume. She wasn't wearing a lot, but he had always had a strong sense of smell. Her smile was there too. It looked comical up close, almost clownish. It took his mind off the pain for a minute or two.

"Where are the others?" He wasn't sure he had asked this out loud, but he must have.

"What others?" She had a puzzled look on her face for a second. "There here," she said. "Why, there's Mr.--."

He groaned. That stopped her. She had backed away now. He saw--no that's not it. He didn't actually see them. He could almost see them. They were aware of him. And he knew they were there. They were there, lingering in the background. They were all around, hovering. He knew they were there somewhere. They weren't close enough really for him to see, but he sensed them. They were getting

The Early Ones

closer. What were they waiting on? They got nothing when he was gone. They had been there since way back. Yes, some of them were the early ones. Early bird gets the worm, he thought. And that's just what he would be soon, very soon. He would disintegrate into dust or whatever. His flesh would rot, his skin receding. He could see it like they showed on those medical T. V. shows, or the C. S. I. shows. The time-lapse camera. Everything would be speeded up. That's certainly how he saw it now. His flesh rotting in record time off the bones. He could see a smile forming, as the flesh melted back, exposing skeletal teeth. An eerie smile. He forgot for a second that it was his own skeleton, or would be. Soon, very soon. A jolt of pain brought him back into the room. The nurse was still there, ever smiling. Her teeth weren't showing, not like the skull, his skull, his future self. But her smile was there. Her smile was all window dressing. Her lips were a bit compressed, and the small crease across her forehead gave things away. She was a little worried that this was it. He knew it wasn't, at least not this very minute. He guessed that she wasn't a bad person. How could she be? He didn't imagine anyone could work where she worked, here, if they were truly a bad person. He sighed. The sigh was a little forced on his part, for her sake. It was his window-dressing. And the crease disappeared, almost, from her forehead. He was still in pain, but the pain was lessening. Perhaps she had administered some more morphine. He hoped.

***

He came up out of the blackness. How long he had been there he couldn't say. It was the land of nothing, apparently. Nothing he could see or hear. Or maybe there was something, something he couldn't remember. A whole lot of things could have gone on during the time of the blackness. Maybe he just remembered it as such, as blackness. And as he was swimming up out of it, the blackness. And his swimming was only how he thought of it. But as he swam up out of the blackness, on the outskirts, before coming all the way to the surface, there would be things. Memories, his life. He was back trudging through the snow, a five-year old, and this time it wasn't early morning, but late afternoon, or perhaps early evening. There was a blackness, like a curtain, hanging above the brightness of the snow. He could hear his sister, Carrie, holler. "Ooh, that one Dad."

The Early Ones

She was pointing and jumping up and down. Another sister joined in. He looked up from the brightness of the snow, not knowing where he had been. Had he been in the darkness? Was it the same blackness that he had come up from now. As a child he didn't think about such things, or he supposed a child didn't think of such things. Things just were. Like the smile on his father's face as he asked, "You sure?" And then the chopping started. The axe would swing and bite. Once, twice, and then again and again. He was small enough, close enough, that he could see the small chips of wood, and could taste the little bit of wood dust that had landed on his lips. His Dad had cautioned him to stay back, but it was impossible. He would inch closer and closer. It was automatic, just something he did. He could taste the sweet taste of the tree, smell the evergreen scent. Moving closer was part of it, getting closer to the action. And soon the tree was down and being dragged through the snow. There was excitement, laughter. The tree would then be lashed to the top of the dark green Hudson. He would be riding in the front seat and feel the strong blowing heat. He would look up and see his Dad, the large plaid maroon colored wool coat, the gray hat with the earflaps. He could smell his Dad's pipe, see the smoke rising up. And there would be laughter on the ride home. Then there was the comfort of the home, warm and inviting, and arguing over who got to hang which bulbs. And then magically, the tree would be standing and lit. It would be bright and majestic, as all things were then. And then it was merely a matter of the wait for Santa. And while awaiting Santa's arrival, he would lay on the kitchen floor, legs half under the table, looking at his little golden book of Zorro. He could smell the cinnamon rolls being baked, by his mother. The book had a bright golden, or yellow cover. Is there a moon behind the man and horse? A picture of Zorro, in any case, dressed in black. His cape is flowing, black on top and red underneath, a bright red, standing starkly out from the black. And Zorro is on his black horse, the horse rearing up. The kitchen is bright and cheery, warm. To a child, all things have a vividness, a brightness to them. There is color, a color so vivid it can't be explained, at least not to an adult. The only time there is no color is when watching television. Everything is black and white on the screen. But the pictures move. And one doesn't notice after a while about the missing color. The latest Abbott

The Early Ones

and Costello movie, whether the two met a ghost or Frankenstein it didn't much matter; the story was still enjoyable. And Zorro is there too. But all else is color. And later, years later, the television was in color too, at least at the neighbor's house. But it was a strange color, and one had to choose between a greenish, or a reddish-orange glow. And the blotches of color, he remembered, would lag behind, or follow Tarzan, Ron Ely, around the screen as the man ran and swung through the trees. Were the blotches of color really that swimmy? But all else, besides the T. V. is clear. The vision is there. The color is blindingly bright. And every adult could go back and experience it again. They could experience it, just as he was experiencing it now. They could swim up out of the darkness and find color. He imagined some did in the end. Some experienced the vividness. But then again, there were probably the others who stayed in the darkness, stayed where it was black. Where there was nothing. Or was there nothing? Death. Death was there. Was death the blackness? Or was death the other side of blackness? Did the blackness only separate life from death? These were questions he couldn't answer, at least not yet. Soon, he thought. Soon. But once he could answer the questions, who would be there to listen? Would there be anyone? A lot of people went. Hell, everybody went. Always, the blackness was there. But would each person have their own separate blackness? He guessed so, because if there were others there in the blackness, there would have to be light to see them. And in that case, there would be no blackness, so it couldn't be called blackness. Or perhaps others were there, believing they were alone because there was no sound. Everyone was waiting quietly, maybe, but for what? Enlightenment of some sort? He had to laugh. He would be there soon enough. He tried to go back to the Christmas tree, the one in the snow, still attached to the ground, still tethered to life. He guessed there was life there. Yes, of course there was. All plants are alive, all plants, trees, etc. So the live tree, that's what he wanted to get back to. He wanted to smell the smell again. He wanted to see the chips flying, the tiny bits of wood particles flying through the air. He wanted to lick the wood dust off his lips. He wanted to call it sawdust, but it wasn't, was it? Not technically. A saw hadn't been used. A saw came later. The saw was for evening off the bottom of the tree so the tree could stand up straight in the stand.

The Early Ones

It was just the axe now. He could hear it, but couldn't find it. He couldn't get back to the tree, the live one. He couldn't get back to his father and sisters, not now. The sounds of the chopping axe stopped completely. Nothing. Not the blackness. Other memories floated up, not quite as vivid, but there. No, now he was sitting on a branch in his makeshift tree house. The wind was howling. It was March. He was sitting on the branch listening to the wind whipping against his weird, triangular shaped tree house. It was just boards nailed to the branches in a haphazard way. There were cracks between them. It was a very small space, but it was his. It was nice. It was his own place. He could sit here and let his mind wander. Though he didn't see it at the time. He couldn't say now whether he thought of it then as his place to let his mind wander. Then he just knew it was a place he could be alone. He laughed now. He laughed as that memory faded. He was always alone. He laughed now as he remembered his teachers, and what they would always write on his report cards. *He does good when he applies himself. For the most part he just stares out the window*. That's what one or two of the cards said. They were right, of course. No question there.

Mark Stattelman

He was always the daydreamer. And where does that get you in life. Nowhere. And yet, that's how it was. That's who he was. Always the daydreamer. When he was sitting alone in his cramped little space of a tree house, listening to the wind whipping around, he was a dreamer. He could hear the wind whistling through the cracks between the boards. It would brush up against him, like errant, exploring fingers, caressing his cheeks and tugging at his jacket, and then passing on. Was it nudging his thoughts, pulling him in one direction or another? Was it trying to wake him up, show him things, things that others couldn't see? His thoughts could fly. He could go places then. He had discovered Jules Verne. He could go all over the world then, traveling with Phileas Fogg and Passepartout. And before that it was with Captain Nemo he had traveled. He had been on the sub, traveled the ocean. Later in life, much later, he had traveled for five weeks in a balloon. And then later still, there was Edgar Rice Burroughs and the Tarzan books. They weren't the dumbed-down version of television and the movies. He could spend hours roaming the African jungle. He lived all the adventure. He was there. And now he thought of Burgess Meredith in the

The Early Ones

Twilight Zone episode, *Time Enough at Last*. Most people were like Meredith's wife in the episode. They didn't understand him. Books. And at the end, when Meredith discovers the library and realizes that he has all the time in the world to read. There he has the books piled in stacks on the front steps. So many books. No one truly understands the joy, or the pain of what happens next. But there is not all the time in the world. There never is. There is never 'Time enough'. And so, now, coming up out of the blackness he sees memories, many memories. Can anyone really know or understand? And with the writing, which came after all the reading of course, things were even more real, as real as life itself. And yet no one seemed to understand. Not many. There would be a few who seemed to. He guessed there were many more out there in the world. There had to be. There were, of course there were! There were tons of books. There was never enough time to read them. That was sad, depressing at times, overwhelmingly so. And the writing, yes the writing. Things were just as vivid then, even more so perhaps. And still no one understood. He wished he had started earlier with the writing. He had written his first story at the age of twenty-eight. And of course, he remembered the little snippet he had written at a very young age. How old had he been then, twelve? Thirteen? The little scene he had written then had been of a tiger moving through the jungle. That's it. That's all it was. He had excitedly run to his parents and showed it to them. They looked at him, a blank stare. They didn't understand. Never would. In any case, after he wrote that first story, and then another, and then another after that, they all kept coming. More and more of them. Not all good, of course. Though some he could go back and read now and they would be better than he had thought. How many stories had he written? Who knows? He should have kept a better count. But he had published, yes, eventually. He had been able to share. He remembered the first few stories he had shared with friends. He had wanted most of all to see, not whether the person liked the story but, whether they could see what he had seen when he had written it. Was the vision clear? Could they see the characters, the action, description, all of it? Most never understood, not really. They would always think he wanted to know whether the story was good or not. That was important, of course, but

The Early Ones

not as important. There would always be more stories. If they didn't like a particular one it didn't matter, there would be more. They could read another one, a different one, written in a different style, a different voice. There would be other characters. So many characters. He couldn't remember them all. They were all alive though. They would pop up and carry the story to its proper end. These characters would all take him places he never knew existed. They would surprise and delight him. Sometimes he could see into their thoughts, know what they were thinking. Other times the thoughts would be hidden from him. He could only watch, record. He was no more than that, a recorder of events. That's all he was. Oh sure, sometimes he would have a say, some input. But mostly it was them. Mostly it was all them. Ahh.

And now, now, as he floated up out of the darkness, into his early memories, now he could see and understand. There they were. He didn't know, but he figured it was all of them. They were there, lingering. Of course, the nurse wouldn't be able to see them. Even if she wanted to, she couldn't. She could read the books, however, if she wanted to do that. He doubted she would. He laughed. They were there. They would always be there, in the world. They were there in the pages, living, breathing. He now envied them. He wanted to be on the page with them, ever static, forever in the world. All anyone had to do was open the book, look on the page and there he would be. But he couldn't. There was no way to put himself on the page. He had life, but it was fleeting. Time, time was a bitch. She was, in some sense, imperceptible. He would love to get his hands on her. He would slip his fingers around her throat and strangle her. But she would always be. And the characters too. He would be gone, but the characters, they would live on, long after he was gone. But would they be alive if no one read them? It is sort of like the question of the tree falling in the woods. If no one is there to hear it, does it make a sound? Well, someone is there, some thing, the small animals, the other trees, plants. They wouldn't, at least not the plants or other trees, have ears to hear, but they could sense the tree falling, crashing. But enough of that. Enough of philosophical questions. That was all unimportant. So, here they were. What were they all waiting for? Were they here to see him off? "C'mon you silly bastards," he muttered. "You silly, lovable creatures you." They

The Early Ones

weren't 'bastards', though, at least not all of them. Nor were they 'creatures.' Not really. Not to him. To him they were people, or beings. But what were they, really? They were his creations. Or were they? Most had materialized without any real thought or action on his part. Well, there was some action. He had to type them up, the characters, the stories they were in. And at first it had been a chore. He remembers the early typewriter. He can distinctly hear the clack and clatter as the little bars (whatever these were called. He had known what they were called once but couldn't think of it now.) as the ends struck the page. The end of the thing would pound against the blank white page and leave the black smudge of a letter. More letters would follow, more words, and then there would be a story, or part of one. Then he would yank the page out of the typewriter when it became full of words, words that had left his mind. His mind would empty and the page would fill. Not really, not usually. Other words and ideas would pop up. It was never ending. He couldn't get them all out fast enough. And if he didn't write for a while, he would become restless and irritable. It was cathartic, something he had to do. But there it was. He could hear the sound of the roller turning as he pulled the full sheet from the typewriter. Was that a buzz? Not quite. A winding sound, sort of. It was a sound that most writers these days wouldn't know. Not in this digital age, as it is called. Now the writer can hear and feel his fingers hitting the keyboard, but that's it. Yes, they can see the letters and words forming on the screen. And what is really beautiful, fantastic actually, is that they can correct things immediately. Yes, just hit the backspace key and then go at it again. It is too easy almost. Perhaps that's why the early stories, the early characters seem a little more special. Not just because they were the early ones, but because there was actual work involved. If the page they were on, had errors, or if they wanted to express themselves a little better, you would have to retype the whole page. Well, there was white-out, of course, but you couldn't send a page with a small glob white-out on it off to the publishers. Nope. Had to be a clean page, clean type, crisp, proper spacing on the borders, the margins, etc. Yep, it was all different then. And thinking back, it was sort of fun reading over the page as you held it in your hands, stopping to cross out a word or two here and there, sometimes writing a better, more suitable word above the scratched out one.

The Early Ones

Hmm. Yes, the early ones were a little more special. That's not to say the newer ones were any less wonderful. Impossible to express it, really. He couldn't quite put his finger on it. And no, they weren't really 'bastards,' that's just the way an old man talks, rough and gruff. A tear rolled down his cheek. He was almost fully up out of the darkness now. He sort of had one foot in his memories. How could he not have? And here they were, they all stepped forward out of the darkness. They weren't demons, lingering on the edges of life. They were all friends. Dare he use the word 'creations'? They were, in a sense, his creations, but they were more. They were friends. Somehow, they were a part of him, and yet not. There is really no way to understand it unless you are a writer, he thought. Here they were. He was smiling now. Here comes Francesca, the little girl from the wall. She has left her parapet, where she sits feeding the pigeons while waiting on her next mark. She was a very early one. And there is the bartender from *Eternal Bar*. That toothy grin. And the redheaded woman from the same story. All her bracelets, he can hear them rattle as they hit the bar top. She is here now. She smiles and waves. And all the others, so many others. Far too many to count.

There is Lorrine, with her big ass combat boots. She hasn't grown an inch. She begrudgingly smiles. He can tell she doesn't want to, or at least she is pretending that she doesn't. And the woman with the Jiminy cricket tattoo on her arm, she steps out of the darkness, pushing through the crowd. The newer characters are here too, not any clearer than the earlier ones, but not any less clear either. They are here, all here. The tears flow from the man's eyes. The writer, that's what he was. But--

"Dad. Daddy, it's me. It's me, Carol. I just got in, flew in from Paris. Todd will be here soon. He's flying in from L. A. He'll be here soon." She looks down at the little girl at her side. "You remember your uncle Todd, don't you sweetie? And this is your Grandpapa." She starts the statement in French and then laughs and shakes her head. "Probably not," she says, using English now. "You were just a baby when we saw him last. Both of them. But we've got photos. And I've sent photos." She looks again at the man. There is a loving, caring look on her face. He can't tell if it is real. It seems fixed in place, much like the nurse's smile. "I spoke to aunt Carrie on the phone. Don't know if she's going to make it. She's having trouble getting around. . ."

The Early Ones

The man feels the nurse pull his blanket up and tuck it around him. He senses that she is smiling now. He looks at the woman speaking to him. "Who are you?" he asks. The woman stares blankly at him. Only silence hangs between them. "Are you one of the early ones?" He can't honestly decide. Her mouth is open now, but no words are forthcoming. She does seem vaguely familiar. She's not as clear as the others. The others are stepping back, moving back into the shadows, out to the edges, lingering again. He feels the pain grow stronger. He wants to go into the blackness and rest, maybe come up and visit again later. He especially likes the early ones, but he truly does love all of them. These newcomers have him puzzled, however. They seem like interlopers of sorts, not real. Not real at all. They are of no substance. He feels like if he turned the page, they would disintegrate, fall apart and disappear. He feels the paper beneath his fingers and grasps the page, turns it. He can hear the shuffle of the page as it turns. He's quite sure they will be gone if he turns the page back and looks again. Somehow, he senses there is no point to that. He wants to move on. He hears the typewriter clacking away in the darkness. He sees the brightness of the white page, the strike of the end of the little rod. He still can't remember the name of it. It thumps the page and falls back, the end leaving a black smudge, a letter. He feels his fingers on the keys. The clattering continues as words form across the page. He senses the characters stepping forward again, out of the shadows. The woman who was annoying him earlier is gone. He was sure she didn't mean to be annoying. But he honestly didn't have time for her. Time is moving swiftly onward, fleeting, fleeing. He hears a whisper, then the voice grows. Quote marks thump onto the page. A word follows. A couple of seconds later there is a whole sentence. The ending quote thumps, sounding just like the opening one. Ah, dialogue. What? He asks. Ah, he's never seen this character before. Yes, yes. He smiles, his fingers riding the keys confidently. As usual, he isn't really that aware of his fingers moving. There is only the vague sense of them. The page disappears and a whole scene presents itself. He can't seem to get it down fast enough. He only hopes he has enough time. He's quite sure now that the woman from earlier wasn't one of the early ones. But he still wasn't sure she was one of the later ones either. That was the rub. Yet she did seem vaguely familiar, just not

The Early Ones

familiar enough to ring a bell. The typewriter dings and, he pushes the lever to advance the roller, the paper, and shift back to the left side of the page. He wonders for a second why he's back on the old typewriter. Well, guess it just feels right for this story, more comfortable. He will catch hell with the errors though. So far there didn't seem to be any. But he hadn't really taken time to read through it yet. He was, after all, just getting started.

MYRA'S WEDDING

Myra had been feeling very strange as of late. Now was not the time to be questioning things; And yet, here she was, doing just that. She stood looking at John. It was their wedding day—her wedding day. It was a day she had looked forward to all of her life. She was quite sure she had looked forward to the day . . . isn't that how it was supposed to be? Shouldn't all girls, young ladies look forward to their wedding day. Myra suddenly had a lot of questions. Why was John looking so stilted? She wanted to ask him, but couldn't. There the two of them stood, at the altar. The preacher had just pronounced them husband and wife and John had stepped forward and put the ring upon her finger. And she had done the same with regard to him. The preacher had stepped back after pronouncing them husband and wife. They had kissed. She knew all of this. It had all happened, right? It had to have happened, all of it, whether she could remember it happening or not. It had to have happened. It was the only logical thing. Why else would the two of them be standing in this very spot? But now, now she was having her doubts. How could she be having doubts. At one point, she must have been totally sure, sure of herself, sure of him. She had to have been. And too, she was now having thoughts, strange thoughts. All of this seemed like it had happened before, all of it. Déjà vu? Over and over again, yes, that's how it seemed.

But why was she questioning it all now? Why today? Her feelings seemed extra strong today, and yet extra strange also. Myra had no doubts that there was a God, and that God was looking down upon them today. There was a higher power, she could feel the presence. She felt the presence so very

Myra's Wedding

strongly. She could almost visualize that presence peering down upon them. So why wasn't she happy? Why did she feel as though she was just waking up from some weird dream? She had the feeling that the dream had played out over and over again, that her wedding was a never-ending affair. And she had noticed something else, just as the room started to spin; that there was a small spot on John's cheek. It looked as though his skin had peeled off, or flaked away. The spot was just on his cheek. The flesh was gone and the spot, which now looked metallic in the lights . . . was odd to her. It seemed so unnatural. She wanted to let go of his hands and reach up to feel the spot. She couldn't. He had her hands gripped tightly. She suddenly felt fear. She didn't know where this feeling was coming from, but it must have been there all along. This fear rose up within her, from somewhere deep inside. This fear turned to terror. Myra wanted to shriek in terror at all of it. Not only did she feel as though she was making a mistake, she felt that all of it was wrong. The whole setting appeared fake, unnatural. John did not seem real to her. He was frightening, especially with the flesh missing from his cheek. He wouldn't release her hands. All she wanted to do was escape. She couldn't. The music had started instantaneously. The lights came on and the music started and the room spun. The room was spinning the whole time . . . and the music. Suddenly Myra couldn't stand the music. She felt it had played over and over again. She was sick of it. Still the room spun. The two of them spun around. And what's worse, things seemed to slow down, as though everything was happening in slow motion. It all felt so mechanical, stilted. Myra felt as though she was on a merry-go-round; She and John both. He held her as they spun. He wouldn't let go. It was almost as though he needed her to keep his balance. She wanted to scream. "Let go! Let go! I hate you! I no longer want to be here!"

And then the lights went out. All was dark. Suddenly everything was pitch black. Myra stood panicking. She tried to pull away. There was something else . . . just before the blackness she heard someone call out. A woman's voice had called out, from somewhere. Myra didn't know where the voice had come from, but it was somewhere distant. "Julia," the voice had called. And then the blackness. The music had stopped, and the room had stopped spinning, just as the darkness fell upon them. Myra

Myra's Wedding

stood there now, frightened. She felt nothing but terror now. The silence. The darkness was complete, and the silence was deafening. And still John held onto her. He wouldn't let go. She screamed at the top of her lungs. She struggled mightily. She broke away . . .

***

The nine-year old girl bounded down the stairs, her blonde hair flopping. "Julia," her mother called. "Dinner is ready—Oh, there you are."

"I heard you," Julia said.

"Did you wash your hands?"

"Ah--" She groaned and went down the hallway to the bathroom. She wasn't angry at having to wash her hands, or at her mother. She was simply irritated with herself, really. Her mother had hollered so . . . and she had just come running down. She hadn't thought about it. She washed, and went back into the dining room.

Julia helped her mother bring dishes from the kitchen. She even helped toss the salad. "Where's dad?" she asked. The door opened about that time and her father came into the house. He had just arrived from work.

"There are my girls," Julia's father said. "And dinner is all set. What more could a man ask for?" He placed a loving hand atop Julia's head, and then stepped over to her mother and gave her mother a kiss on the cheek. Julia's mother was carrying a hot bowl, and had oven mitts on. Still she presented her cheek for Julia's father to kiss. He carried his briefcase in one hand. "I'll be back in a jiffy," he said. "Just let me get cleaned up." He disappeared down the hall.

Julia and her mother then seated themselves at the table. They were waiting on Julia's father before they started eating. "Did you finish your homework?" Julia's mother asked.

"Yes, mother, I did."

"So, what were you doing?"

"Nothing, Julia said, "just playing with my music box."

Julia's father entered the room and sat down. They said grace and then ate. At the end of dinner, her mother stood up and took the plates away, carrying them into the kitchen and setting them on the counter. A couple of minutes passed before she re-entered the room. When she returned, she was smil-

Myra's Wedding

ing wide. She carried a birthday cake, Julia's birthday cake. There were nine candles glowing atop the cake. Julia's mother set the cake on the table directly in front of Julia. Julia's father sat grinning. "My little girl's growing so fast I almost don't even recognize her anymore."

"Make a wish, sweetie," her mother said. Her father watched her.

Julia sat for a minute. She already knew what she wanted, more than anything else in the world. She wished for a life like her parent's had. She knew that her mother and father loved each other unquestioningly. She only hoped she could find a love like that. And she would have the perfect wedding . . . just like her music box. Julia had named the music box couple, Myra and John. That was exactly how Julia wanted her wedding to be. She wanted to be Myra, and to marry John . . .

***

Julia lay across her bed. She had just finished chatting on her phone with her friend Erin. Erin had to go, so they said goodbye and hung up. Julia tossed the phone aside. She lay there, staring up at the ceiling. Her music box was still on the bed, just where she had left it when her mother had called her down to dinner. She hadn't paid much attention to it for the past few years. But this afternoon she had picked it up off the dresser and opened the box, having first wound the key. Julia reached over and pick up the box now. She wound the key and opened the lid. The music played, and the small altar turned, but there was only one figure. John was the only figure standing. He spun around. Julia frowned. She didn't think she had thrown the box down hard enough to have broken anything. Besides, the bed was soft. Nothing would have broken. But still. She saw Myra lying at the shorter edge of the rectangular box. Myra's hands appeared to be higher than they had been. Surely Myra's hands had been lower down. John had been holding Myra's hands. Now though, Myra's hands were covering her face. Strange, thought Julia. She picked up the small figure of Myra and looked closely at it. Nothing else appeared different. Still frowning, she lay Myra on the bed. Julia was sitting up now, looking down at John. He seemed so lonely, standing there, turning all by himself. Julia thought of her wish now. She smiled and shook her head. If only, . . . she thought."

***

Myra's Wedding

"Julia, are you up?" It was morning, and Julia's mother stood at the bottom of the stairs. There was no answer. She hollered again. "Julia!" She looked at her watch.

"Okay."

"Shoot," Julia's mother mumbled to herself. I'm going to be late if I don't hurry. She knew she had agreed to show the Anderson couple the house this morning. They had wanted to meet early. "Honey," she hollered up to Julia. "I've got to run. Your father has already gone." She grabbed her coat off of the back of the chair and put it on. She went to the door and looked at herself in the mirror that hung on the wall next to the door. She brought her fingers up and brushed a couple of strands of hair up off of her forehead. She pursed her lips together, and ran a pinky fingernail around the edge of her mouth. "Don't fall back asleep, sweetie! And don't be late for school." She opened the door and then went out, pulling it shut behind her. Only silence hung in the house for a few minutes.

Slowly, Julia's bedroom door opened. Myra peeked out. She was naked. She was a full-grown woman. There was no way she was going to fit into a nine-year old girl's clothes. Not that she wanted to, anyway. She went down the hallway and entered the master bedroom. She opened the closet and found a dress. She held it up in front of her naked body. Myra was similar in build to Julia's mother, but the dress wouldn't be an exact fit. She slipped into it all the same. She looked at herself in the mirror of the dresser. God, my hair, she thought. She spotted a brush on the vanity. She picked it up and brushed her long brown tresses. It'll have to do, she thought, tossing the brush back onto the dresser top. She had to hurry and get out of the house. She rounded the corner and headed back into the hall. She heard the front door open. Shit, she thought. She froze.

Julia's father was coming up the stairs. He looked surprised when he saw her. She didn't know what to say. A puzzled look crossed his face. "Who are you?" he asked.

Myra was startled. "I'm--" she was about to say that she was Julia's friend Erin's mother. Erin and her mother had bought the music box for Julia a couple of years earlier; A birthday gift. So, she knew them. She had seen them because they had played the box. At that time, Myra had thought they had just been faces in the crowd, at the wedding. Now she knew better. Suddenly she realized Julia's father

Myra's Wedding

might have met Erin's mother at some point. "I'm Erin's aunt," she said.

"Oh," said Julia's dad. He stood looking at her. Then he glanced at his watch. "I forgot my cell phone." He went on into the master bedroom and picked the phone up off the night table. He rounded the corner into the hall, slipping the phone into his suit coat pocket. He still looked puzzled. Myra stood frozen, wishing he would move on past. She had just pulled Julia's door all the way closed. Julia's dad stopped.

Myra realized he needed more of an explanation. "Julia overslept," she said. She paused. She realized he needed more. "She phoned Erin and asked if she could get a ride. Erin's mom was busy, so I volunteered to give the girls a ride. She smiled at him and held out her hand. I'm Myra, by the way."

"Oh. Bill," Julia's dad responded. He shook her hand. "Nice to meet you." There was a short, awkward pause. Bill looked at his watch. "Well, I've got to get going," he said. He smiled. Myra smiled back. He moved on past, starting down the steps. He stopped and looked back. "I can give the girls a ride."

Myra's smile froze and then dropped away. She felt like it shattered when it hit the floor. God, she thought. "It's okay," she said suddenly. "I'm already here." She shrugged her shoulders, giving her friendliest smile.

"True," he said. "And I'm running late. See you." He gave a slight wave of his hand and started down the stairs again. He stopped and turned, looking back once more. "You know," he said. "My wife's got a dress just like that."

"Really?" Myra smiled.

"Beautiful, classy women dress alike, I guess. Or at least have the same taste." He paused for a second longer.

Is he coming on to me? Myra thought. She looked at him. He smiled again. I wish, she thought. Then, no, wait a minute . . . no, no.

Bill sort of shook his head and continued on his way. Myra waited until she heard the front door close. She fell against the wall, thinking she might pass out. Then she had another thought. She hoped he didn't notice the fact that there was no car on the street out front. She waited a little longer. He didn't come back.

Myra's Wedding

After a couple more minutes, Myra ran back into the master bedroom and found a suitcase. She found a few more dresses and stuffed them into the suitcase. She tried a pair of jeans, pulling them up beneath the dress. There was a little more room in the hips than she needed, but they would work. At least they weren't too small. She closed the case and then ran back into Julia's room. She picked up Julia's cell phone off the bed and ordered a Lyft. She needed to hurry. She tossed the phone back onto the bed. She picked up the suitcase and started out of the room. She stopped. She went over to the bed and picked up the music box. She opened the lid. Nothing happened. She looked and saw Julia, the nine-year old little girl in a wedding dress that was way too large for her. John was holding the little girl's hands. He had the same expression that he always wore. Julia appeared happy. Still, why no music? Then Myra saw the key on the back of the box. She wound it. The music played and John and Julia twirled around in wedded bliss. Myra watched for a couple of seconds. A horn sounded outside. She dropped the box onto the bed and picked up the suitcase, hurrying out of the room. She ran down the stairs and out the front door. She climbed into the waiting car. It pulled away.

Upstairs, the music played. It only stopped momentarily when the key got caught on the blanket. Slowly, the key turned. The music sounded slow and warped; then the key worked loose and the music started playing properly again and then played out. The lid was still open. The couple stood at an odd angle. Julia was looking up at John. He held onto her, keeping her from falling backward. Beyond his shoulder, Julia could see where her wallpaper met the ceiling of her room. She hoped she and John would be happy together. John stared back at her. He seemed happy. The small place on his cheek where the paint had chipped away didn't bother her too much. She had dropped the box one afternoon a long time ago. The box had slipped out of her hands and the corner of the dresser caught John's cheek before the whole thing tumbled to the floor. She wasn't happy that it happened. But she felt she could get used to it. After all, she had played it many times and was able to overlook the tiny glitch. Of course, the spot looked a little larger from this perspective. She looked into his eyes. He continued smiling at her. His blue eyes appeared full of love, just for her.

FOOTPRINTS

Karen had seen the footprints in the sand as she walked along the beach. The sun had come up and presented them to her. She thought of the symbolism. There had been a card, or saying, something that she couldn't exactly remember. Had it been a religious saying? Something about God? She smirked and shook her head. It would come to her. Then she stopped abruptly. The footsteps ended. Right there in the sand, they stopped. She stood staring down at them, the prints. She watched as the ocean waves rolled in and over her bare feet. The waves rolled and tumbled, sliding across her toes. The foamy, frothy, gurgling essence shifted the dark sand before her. As the waves receded, sliding back over her feet, back into the sea, the footprints disappeared. She turned and looked behind her. The prints had all disappeared. She had followed along beside the impressions in the sand, wondering only vaguely at first, who might have left them. Then she had wondered about the card, or saying . . . and then she simply stood at the spot where the prints ended completely. And she then saw the sand go smooth again, right before her eyes. But who? How? Perhaps someone had walked along just minutes before her. She always liked to wake up early and walk along the beach. She enjoyed the silence, only the sound of the waves. She was contemplative, at peace. This was exactly what she needed. Perhaps someone else needed the same thing. They had just trod along the beach a little earlier than she had. The only thing was . . . the waves hadn't washed the prints away before she had come along, which was very odd. Whoever it had been would have had to have been walking just a minute or two before her. She looked down the beach ahead. No one. She looked behind her. No one. The beach was deserted. The ocean breeze whisked in and brusquely pushed her hair, whipping it around and

Footprints

across her face. She pulled her hair back, tucking it behind her ear. She felt a chill, and gathered the oversized cardigan closely about her. It was suddenly cool. Clouds blocked the rising sun, curled about it. Karen heard a gull squeal in the distance. She turned and started back toward the bungalow. She shivered again. The wind whipped harder, feeling like sandpaper scraping across her face.

***

Nothing seemed out of place. The small bungalow, or beach house appeared normal, ordinary enough. The place was basically immaculate. The bed was made in the bedroom. Nothing unusual. On the table in the dining room was a mug half full of coffee. There was a legal pad and pencil next to it, and a partial ream of white paper. A typewriter was on the table. The typewriter sat directly in front of the dining chair that was pulled partway out. In the typewriter was a piece of paper, rolled beneath the platen. One word had been typed: Footprints. The typewriter hummed, still plugged into the outlet on the wall. Nothing was disturbed, or out of the ordinary . . .

***

Mark Stattelman

Karen doubled over with the pain, right there on the beach. She felt the stabbing, searing cuts and jabs. The waves washed onto the beach. The waves were unrelenting. So was the pain. The miscarriage. The baby, the dying baby, the pain and anguish, the loss had been almost unbearable. Almost, she thought. No, not almost. It had been completely unbearable. Even after the fact, even then, it had been too much to bear. The psychologist agreed that Karen needed to get away. The physician, her regular doctor had said that there was nothing physically wrong. He had told her that she was healthy. Karen and Richard could try again. They would try again. But she couldn't. There was the pain, still. It was there. It came and went, washing over her. Richard had been understanding at first. But then, after a time, he suggested that it was all in her mind. He agreed that she needed to get away, take some time. And so, she came to the beach house. It was off season, though that didn't matter too much, because their section of beach was somewhat secluded. Their house was the last one. Not many people came down this far, even when the crowds were visiting. Beyond their house was the stretch of beach that extended a good distance, and then there was a large

Footprints

section of woods. Karen wasn't exactly sure how far the woods went. She guessed it went on for a few miles. She had ventured into the woods on a few occasions, but stopped and returned home when it became too thick and scary. Yes, scary, eerie. She had a weird feeling at times, as though she were being watched. She could feel eyes staring at her, from the woods. But perhaps it was just her mind playing tricks. Maybe she was being paranoid.

Karen loved her early morning walks on the beach. She would get up early, just before sun up. Often, she made a pot of coffee and sat down to write. She had work to do still, but lately she had abandoned that. Her laptop battery had died. She didn't much care. Then she had remembered the old typewriter, from college days. It was old then, even. No one used typewriters anymore. Why would they? She had written her first book on that typewriter, though, or at least most of it. Then she had had to scan the work into the computer. That had been a real pain, a lot of work. It was extra work. Why? Well, for some reason, she felt more creative using the old-fashioned typewriter. She felt more like an old-fashioned writer, a real writer. Thoughts came clearly. Except with the footprints. No thoughts came about those. She needed thoughts about the footprints. She wanted answers. Since she had seen the footprints the other day, things had changed. She felt as though she must surely be losing it. The meds, perhaps, were causing her to hallucinate. She had called the psychologist, and her doctor. Both had asked if she had been drinking while being on the meds, lately. No, she had said. Nothing except a couple of glasses of wine. But the footprints had shown up. The footprints, and then the small child. Karen had simply first dreamed of the little girl. Or perhaps she had only been on the edges of sleep, coming up out of the dreams. But there the little girl was. Karen walked along the beach, the little girl beside her, walking with her. The only thing that didn't make sense was that this little girl would be older than the unborn child Karen had lost. They had lost. Richard had lost the baby also, yes, but his loss was different. He didn't feel the actual physical pain. No, there was no way he could feel the loss in the same way.

   Karen looked forward to her walks every morning. Sometimes the little girl would be walking with her, and sometimes not. It was weird, scary. Not scary like the woods. The woods were different. The

Footprints

woods would be terrifying. She wouldn't go there. The scariness of the beach was with regard to the little girl. And at times, the child would be comforting, not scary at all. Karen, as long as she didn't question the girl's reality, or her own sanity—well, then the little girl wasn't scary at all. The two of them would be together. The little girl would look up and smile. She could hear the girl's voice, the little tiny voice that said "Mommy." Karen would be happy and warm when she looked down at the girl. Then Karen would look up and away. She would look at the rising sun. Something kept her from the woods. She tried not to let her attention go to the woods. But there would be something, someone, pulling her attention toward the woods—pulling *her* toward the woods. Karen resisted. And then Karen would look down and the little girl would be gone. Nowhere. Karen would look down the beach and it would be empty. And sometimes Karen felt that she had simply walked on and left the little girl behind. That little presence, the little bundle of joy, the joy that she would never know, was nowhere to be seen. But the prints. The small prints would be there in the sand, at least before they got washed away by the waves. The waves rolled up and then receded, erasing the prints, removing the last remnants of the little girl. And then the prints were larger. Today the prints had been an adult. But Karen hadn't seen the adult. It scared her. All of it scared her. Was it the medication? Was it the drugs she had been on for the depression? She had to be hallucinating. Yes, that was it. None of it was real, nothing was real. The woods were real. The trees were actually there. There was no denying that. But what about the presence, the ominous presence that lingered within the woods? The woods were begging for her attention. She dared not look. She dared not go there. Something evil was there. And what of the sense of being watched. She looked around. The beach was empty. She looked down. No prints. Dammit, she thought. Footprints. What was it about the footprints? Why couldn't she think of the saying? What had it been? It was on a card. Yes, but was it a poem? A prayer? Something about God? Karen felt the pain now, the immense, tremendous pain. It was stabbing her. She doubled over. She curled up. She felt the coldness of the water as it swirled around her and eased beneath her. Karen felt the dampness, the cold and shifting sands . . .

***

Footprints

It had been three weeks. They hadn't found the woman. Karen Evans was missing. Richard Evans had called the police. They had canvassed the homes in the area. They had looked all up and down the beach. No one had seen her. But they, all of the residents along the beach, had agreed that Karen Evens had pretty much kept to herself. Most of them had met her and Richard Evans. There hadn't been any new people moving into the area along the beach. There had been no strangers lurking about that anyone had noticed. But still the woman had disappeared. She had vanished, into thin air. Detective Ed Gieren stood in the beach house. He wasn't sure why he was still standing there. He wasn't sure why he had come back. They had been all over the place. They had questioned everyone. They had searched everywhere. He stood looking out the patio door. He looked at the ocean, the sun had arisen. A beautiful sight. He wondered vaguely whether he and his wife could maybe afford a place like this in a few years, when he retired. Gieren sighed. Probably not. He turned around, letting his eyes roam about the room. Nothing. He wandered over to the table. There, the half-filled mug still sat. A funky substance was starting to grow on the surface of the liquid. Hadn't someone tested for DNA? Hadn't they taken a sample at least, checked for poisons? Then he remembered, the woman was not dead, at least as far as anyone knew. She could have just met someone and taken off. Perhaps Karen Evans had abandoned her life, her husband. There had been problems between the two. The husband had admitted that there had been problems. Richard Evans had told him about the loss of the baby, and the rest. Evans had told them about his wife's depression, the medication to relieve that depression. They had been to see the psychologist, along with Karen's regular physician. Nothing. Had Karen committed suicide? If so, why wouldn't she have just done it here? There were no signs of it, and definitely no body. Had she taken pills and then wandered into the ocean? Still, no body. The body would have washed up onto the beach. Probably. It could have been pulled out, he guessed, or gotten hung on something. But no. No signs of pills. Well, nothing other than the regular prescription, and all of those, the proper number accounted for from the time the prescription had been filled.

Footprints

The detective sighed. Something would turn up. He had other cases. Perhaps Karen Evans would turn up, alive. Maybe she had just needed to get away. She would contact her husband. Gieren stared down at the table. What if Karen Evans showed up and didn't know anyone was looking for her. Suppose she contacted no one? Maybe she wouldn't even contact her husband, depending on the circumstances. He decided to leave his card on the table, just in case. He searched his pockets. Nothing. He had none of his cards on him. For whatever reason, he hadn't stuck any new ones in his pocket. He remembered having given the last one out the other day. He had plenty back at the office, but nothing with him. He glanced at the pad and pencil. That would have been the natural thing to do, write his name and number there. He didn't. For whatever reason, he switched on the typewriter. It had been humming the last time he had been here, but now it was off. He would type a note, telling her to get in touch. He leaned down to type. It certainly wasn't going to be a long note, so he didn't need to sit. He felt a little funny. For some reason he felt like he would be invasive if he sat in the chair. He wasn't sure why he felt this way. After all, he and the others had all searched through Karen Evans's bedroom. They had looked through her dresser drawers. He had seen her underwear, her lingerie. He brushed the thoughts away, not allowing his mind to linger on the image of her undergarments. Still, he didn't sit down. He looked at the word that Karen had typed: *Footprints*

  Detective Gieren started typing. For whatever reason, playfulness? He had no idea why, but he typed the words: *in the sand*. He typed these words right after footprints. He couldn't remember any more. He couldn't remember the rest of it, the poem, or whatever it was. He stopped typing. He didn't type his note. He frowned and stood up, trying to remember the rest of the saying. He walked over to the patio door again. The rest of the poem, or whatever, skirted about in his mind. It lingered around the dark edges. Footprints, he thought. He stood looking out at the beach. He wanted to wander along the beach and look. Ridiculous, he thought. They had been all up and down the beach. It would be nice, he thought as he stood there looking out. It certainly would be convenient if he could just walk out onto the beach and follow Karen Evans's footprints. Would the prints lead directly to her? Would

Footprints

she be dead? Alive? He started to smile to himself. He froze. There was a sound behind him. He shivered. A chill. A presence. He felt it. He was afraid to turn around. He turned anyway. There was no other choice. The typewriter was typing. All of its own accord. Detective Gieren moved toward the table, slowly . . .

***

in the sand, Karen thought. Yes. Yes! That was it, footprints in the sand . . . her mind was freed. Something had broken loose. Somehow. There was pain. Tremendous pain. She felt the stabbing, the slicing of the blade. The blade. Or no, was it the branches that she felt? She was no longer on the beach—she was in the woods. She was running through the woods. It was night, all was dark. There was the sallow, sickly moon. She could see it. She got snatches of vision. It came to her in jolting waves, like the pain. The moon. High up, between the branches of the trees. She was then caught up in the sounds of her breath as she ran. Someone was chasing her. She was running through the woods. She moved as fast as she could, but not fast enough. The branches cut and scraped her. She fell. She crawled, moving forward, going nowhere. She rose, stumbling, to her feet. She ran, the branches and brambles catching against her, her arms, her sides. There were thick vines and brambles. Where was the beach? Where was the child? She tripped again, and fell. She felt the branches slicing into her, and then the knife. The blade sliced and stabbed. She felt the pain. She now lay on the beach, looking up. She lay in a fetal position, curled, the waves washing up, water pushing through the shifting sands. The sun had come up. It blinded her; and when it receded, she saw the child, the little girl. Her little girl. The child smiled down at her.

***

"We found your wife," said Detective Gieren. "She's dead." He watched as Richard Evans looked shocked. The man's face fell; his mouth dropping open. Richard Evans dropped his head into his hands. Gieren waited. The fluorescent lights buzzed overhead in the interrogation room.

"Wh-where?" Evans asked in a choking sob. "Where? What? No—no. She can't be. She—Karen, Karen can't be dead." He continued sobbing.

The detective waited. He gave Evans enough time, before he continued. "We got a cadaver dog."

Footprints

Evans stopped sobbing. Just for a second, he stopped. His head rose. "Where was she?" he asked.

Gieren looked at Evans. There was a significant pause before he spoke. "The woods," he said. "The ones near the beach, just a short distance from you and your wife's house at the beach." He waited.

Richard Evans sobbed again. This time it was just a short, loud jag of a sob. He stopped and looked up at Gieren. Gieren continued. "Your wife's body wasn't buried very deep. The cadaver dog found the spot easy enough." He sat looking at Evans. Evans looked back at the detective. Anguish was on Evans's face. "What did you do with the child's body?" Gieren asked.

Richard Evans's face suddenly changed. There was immediate shock and surprise. His mouth hung open. He didn't understand. Perhaps they had found another body, someone else besides his wife. Had there been someone else buried in the woods? Was this a mistake? Must be. There had to be some mistake.

"There was a child's shoe in your wife's hand. She was gripping it tightly when she died." Gieren waited. He waited for an answer from Evans. No answer was forthcoming. The man had none. "So, I ask you again--What did you do with the child's body, Mr. Evans?"

I would very much like to thank you for reading these stories. I sincerely hope you enjoyed them. If so, please leave a review. It helps me so, so much. Also, if you enjoyed this book, feel free to check out my other titles:

Fiction:

Dark Tales of the Civil War Series:

Daguerreotype Dreams (Volume One)
I Fear Only the Dogs (Volume Two)
And You Shall Not Live (Volume Three)
The Scarecrow and other stories (volume Four)-- Coming soon.

Novellas:
The Dancing Man
The Children's Home

Other Short Story Collections:

The Soft Eloquence of Neon (Early short stories)

Science Fiction:
The Red Kimono (coming soon)

Nonfiction:
Write Play Love: How I Write Short Stories
Format Your Book: How to format your manuscript for Amazon using Microsoft Word!

You can catch me on Goodreads (one of my favorite hangouts), or visit my website at
www.markstattelman.com

Thank You again!

Mark Stattelman